THE WEDDING WAGER

Regina Duke

PUBLISHED BY:
Regina Duke

The Wedding Wager
Copyright © 2012 Linda White

Print ISBN: 978-0-9858482-1-7
Digital ISBN: 978-0-9858482-0-0
Kindle ASIN: B0094KFI7W

www.reginaduke.com

This book is a work of fiction and all characters exist solely in the author's imagination. Any resemblance to persons, living or dead, is purely coincidental. Any references to places, events or locales are used in a fictitious manner.

Cover design and formatting by Sandra Edwards
(www.sandrawrites.com)
Photos used to make the cover obtained from fotolia.com

Not all of us can do great things. But we can do small things with great love.

~ Mother Theresa

I cannot name everyone who has cheered me on and held me up, for that would take another book. So I will limit myself to the few most involved in my journey thus far. I thank Greg and Karen Gandy, Cindy White, and Vicky Stambaugh. I thank my editor Marian Kelly. And I thank Sandra Edwards, for without her my books might still be languishing in a drawer.

Chapter One

June 1

"THAT'S INSANE! HE CAN'T DO THAT."

Krystal Fineman Wake clutched the handset of her bedside phone until her knuckles whitened and slumped against her pillows. The outburst had cost her. For a moment, she concentrated on breathing. Then she continued.

"That property came down from my great-grandfather."

"Sorry, ma'am," said Zach, "but as ranch foreman I figured it was my duty to let you know the scuttlebutt, even if it was bad news."

Krystal knew that in this day and age, Colorado was not that far from New York, but her old phone made him sound like he was calling from a different planet instead of a different state.

"Thank you, Zach. My husband seems determined to squander my legacy and deprive my children of their rightful due." She paused again for breath.

Zach broke the awkward silence. "I hope you feel better soon, ma'am."

"Me, too. Meanwhile, get the house ready. I'm bringing the children out right away. I've had enough of New York City. It breeds deception."

"Yes, ma'am. Everyone here will be happy to know you're coming. Er, all of 'em? Even Kevin?"

"I'm not sure how, but yes, even Kevin. Especially Kevin. The only way to save the ranch is to have my children fall in love with it, so we'd better act fast. I always suspected that if I died before him, my husband intended to sell it. But I had an ace in the hole. Or I thought I did."

"You mean the trust?"

"Yes. In the early 1900s, young men routinely married early, and the requirement that the male heir be wed before inheriting on his twenty-fifth birthday was not considered a hardship. I'm sure my parents never expected the day would come when a young man would prefer to live single. If he did, then he was clearly, in their minds, not responsible enough to manage the family fortune." Her voice turned bitter. "They meddled in my personal life, too. And look who I ended up with." She paused again to breathe. "Sorry, Zach. I'm rambling. You get the house ready. I have some phone calls to make."

Kevin Wake rolled his six foot four inch frame out of bed and onto the cold linoleum floor of his boarding house room. His single luxury, his iPhone, was ringing. He'd set it on the dresser so he would be forced to get up when the alarm sounded.

He stumbled across the room and grabbed the phone. It wasn't the alarm. He had a call. He stared at the number and fought a wave of panic. There was only one reason his mother's lawyers would call him, and he feared the worst. He answered cautiously.

"Hello?"

"It's your mother," said Krystal.

His panic subsided. "Mom? Why are you calling from Ratigan and Sons?"

"Something is going on behind your back and I want you to have a fighting chance."

Kevin glanced at the clock. "Talk fast, mom. I'll be late for class."

"Stop with the graduate school bull crap, Kevin. I know you're not in the MBA program. I keep sending your allowance because you have a right to it."

Kevin unplugged the iPhone from its charger and checked the mini fridge for a soda. He popped the lid and sat on the single chair in the corner.

"And I keep putting it in the bank, in case you need it back some day. You know I want to make it on my own."

"Let's not fight," said Krystal. "I don't have the energy for it. Besides, your father is the enemy, not me."

"All right," said Kevin. "What's the old man done this time?"

"He has wagered your future away."

"What does that mean?"

"It means he intends to enforce the letter of the trust. It means he will not back down. He wants to control my wealth completely and in order to do that he must wrangle the last hope for your inheritance from your grasp. He has gone so far as to wager that you will fail to meet the terms and allow him to gain complete control. He and his Wall Street buddies are having a gay old time, making book on your eventual misfortune."

"Look, mom, I know he can be a bastard when it comes to money, but Nicholas Ratigan promised us he could get those terms altered in court."

"Your father has his own lawyers, Kevin, and they have countered Ratigan's request. I overheard a conversation he was having with them—"

Kevin interjected, "You mean, you eavesdropped."

"My children's future is at stake. I do what I must. Your father's lawyers will see to it that the requirements of the trust are met to the letter of the law. If you are not legally married by your twenty-fifth birthday, it will all come to me. You know I'm not strong, and my health is not improving. Failure to thrive, they say, which means they have no answers. You must be in a position to take over the inheritance, because if it comes to me, Douglas will find a way to rip it away, and believe me, Kevin, there will be nothing left by the time your brother and sister are of age."

Kevin felt like he'd been hit with a hammer. "I was counting on the Ratigans."

"I know. And I was counting on your father still having a shred of decency left."

"But my birthday is only a month away!"

"I guess you better get busy," said Krystal. "I'm taking Karla and Keegan to the ranch for the summer, and there will be a wedding on June 29th, the day before your birthday. You be there with your bride. And remember it has to be legal and believable. If there is a hint of suspicion, if your father's lawyers get a toehold, they'll hang this up in the courts for years. I have to go." Her voice softened. "I love you, Kevin."

Kevin hung up and began to pace. Ever since he was old enough to know the difference between rich and poor, he'd felt guilty for being a member of the privileged class. His mother came from old money, earned the hard way, but his dad's wealth came from the worst kind of

capitalism and Kevin wanted nothing to do with it. When he told his father how he felt, Douglas Wake's rage turned physical, and when Kevin left for college, he never expected to return.

That's why he lived the way he did, in a one-room convenience apartment. He rode a bicycle to work. He'd made a vow to himself that every penny of the allowance his mother sent him would go into a savings account. He needed to know how to make it on his own. And it had not been easy. Many times he'd been tempted to raid that savings account. He only succumbed once, to pay for his iPhone, his connection to the world.

But now he would have to dip into it for sure. If he was going to attract a bride, even a temporary one, he would need money. He would need to project the same kind of power and wealth that he despised in his father if he was going to find the right kind of woman. But he would have to go about it carefully. He didn't want to attract gold diggers.

He looked at his reflection in the mirror. His square jaw, hazel eyes, and wavy dark hair attracted plenty of dates, but he seldom saw them twice. Besides, that wasn't the kind of girl he could present as a bride. Not even a fake one. He needed a good, wholesome girl who could pass muster as a Wake. He made a disgusted noise. No, he needed a girl who could pass muster as a Fineman, his mother's side of the family. The problem was, the kind of girl he needed was not the kind of girl who would take money to pretend to be his bride.

If it were only his future at stake, he would turn his back and walk away. But his sister Karla and his little brother Keegan had a stake in this as well. Like his mother said, by the time they were old enough to claim their inheritance, his father would find a way to turn all the assets into cash and stuff it into a Swiss bank account, hidden from them until the day he died. If there was any left by then. He'd already managed one legal maneuver after another to gain control of his mother's wealth. The only portion left was that guarded by the trust fund that Kevin could only fall heir to by marrying before his twenty-fifth birthday. It was money from that trust that his mother, as a trustee, was using for his allowance.

So far, Kevin could support himself. But Keegan deserved a chance to go to a good school, and Karla should not be forced to do the kind of menial jobs he had chosen to do in order to get by.

He couldn't turn his back. Like it or not, he was going to have a wedding on June 29th, and he'd better get busy and find a bride.

Chapter Two

MEGAN MULLY STEPPED THROUGH the doors of the University of Washington Medical Center, her home for the last six months, and took a deep breath of fresh Seattle air. For a moment, she closed her eyes and let the sun beat down on her upturned face. It felt good to be outdoors again.

Oh, she'd been allowed outside during her stay, but she always knew she had to go back to her hospital room. Not this time. This time she was free to go anywhere she wanted.

She opened her eyes and gulped.

The only problem was, there was nowhere to go.

Her car had been totaled in the accident that put her in the hospital. She was moving to Seattle when it happened, so she didn't even have an apartment. The job that was waiting for her went to another when she couldn't show up for work. Everything she owned had been in that car, including her cell phone. All gone. But she couldn't pay the cell phone bill anyway, without a job. So it didn't matter.

She looked around at the acres of sidewalk that surrounded the medical center and realized she didn't even know where to catch the bus.

Megan swallowed several times but the lump in her throat threatened to bring tears.

She shook off the loneliness, straightened her shoulders and clutched the battered purse slung over her shoulder. Inside, in her

11

battered wallet, she had exactly forty dollars in cash. Her mother left it with her when she had to return to her father at the mission in Guatemala. There were lots of rewards in missionary work, but none of them were monetary.

The wallet wasn't the only thing in her purse. She could almost feel the dreaded envelope through the bag. As broke and alone as she was, it was that envelope that threatened to fill her with despair. But there was nothing she could do about that at the moment. She braced herself to face her first day of freedom. But without the structure of physical therapy and hospital meals, she realized she had no plan for it.

Well, there was no time like the present to start looking for work. She patted her pockets for change, found a handful of quarters, and bought a newspaper from the box at the corner. She settled on a shady bench and turned to the want ads.

An hour later, the shade had shifted and the pleasant morning sun was turning into a noontime sunburn machine. Just her luck to be released on one of Seattle's rare sunny days. Megan's optimism was wilting in the heat. Column after column was filled with requirements and demands for experience that she did not have. Not one of them wanted a "twenty-four-year-old woman willing to learn, no experience necessary, will provide apartment and car."

She laughed out loud at herself. The chances of finding an ad like that were almost as great as being abducted by aliens and learning she was a princess on another world. She turned the page. There were only two columns left. She might as well read through them all before she spent part of her precious forty dollars on something to eat.

She skimmed along the columns, hunger making her read faster. Journeyman Mechanic? Nope, not qualified. Radiology nurse? Wrong major. Nurse's aide? By golly, she could do that one in her sleep, but the idea of moving from patient to caretaker in the hospital she just left did not appeal to her at all. The rest of the column was mostly clerical. And then there were sales positions. She could not stand on her feet all day, not for a while anyway. Those were out.

She just about gave up hope when the last ad in the last column caught her eye.

At first she thought it was a joke.

"Exceptional opportunity for a young lady, aged 22-25, willing to relocate. Gentleman's personal secretary. Must be of high moral fiber. Lodging and transportation included in generous salary. Personal interviews only." It ended with a phone number.

She read it ten times, trying to figure out what the trick was. But the words did not change. There it was. Gentleman's personal secretary.

She wasn't totally naive. She figured the "personal" part was very personal. But then again, it required "high moral fiber." Goodness knew she had plenty of that. It was almost the only legacy her parents had provided for her before they took up missionary work.

No matter how many times she closed the newspaper and opened it again, the ad was still there.

After half an hour of shifting between too good to be true and sent from God, she decided it wouldn't cost her anything but the price of a phone call. She knew there were pay phones in the lobby of the hospital, so she gritted her teeth and walked back into the megalithic structure she'd been so happy to leave a couple of hours before.

"Hello?" A man answered. He had a nice enough voice, and he didn't sound like an old codger. But this could be an employee, she thought.

"Hi. My name is Megan Mully and I'm calling about the ad in the paper, the one for a gentleman's personal secretary?"

"Yes?"

"Has it been filled yet?"

"No, not yet, Ms. Mully. Would you like to interview for the position?"

"Yes, please."

"Can you be available at two today?"

Megan hesitated. "Well, I can, but..."

"Is there a problem?"

"I have no car. At the moment," she added quickly. She didn't want to sound destitute.

"I'll send a car for you," said the voice.

"May I ask who will be conducting the interview?"

"Certainly. Mr. Kevin Fineman Wake will do the honors. If you'll give me your address, I'll send a driver."

Megan gave him the name of the medical center and the cross street. Then she added, "Oh, by the way, I need to, uh, leave the address of the interview with, with,..." —*with another human being in case you turn out to be a serial killer*— "...with my mother so she won't worry." She cringed. That sounded so stupid!

"Of course. I wouldn't want your mother to worry." He seemed amused, but he gave her an address in the downtown area. At least she thought it was downtown. Her entire six month stay in Seattle had been

spent in the hospital. She only knew the area through television news broadcasts.

"My driver will be there in half an hour."

"Great. Oh! How will I know it's your car?"

"He'll be driving the white limo today." Click.

"Okay, then," said Megan into the dead phone. "The white limo." She replaced the hand set and headed purposefully toward the alcove where the snack food machines stood waiting. "Definitely the white limo," she said in an affected tone. "One never drives black at this time of year." Then she giggled.

A Snickers bar and a can of Coke had her buzzing with sugar by the time the white limo pulled up in front of the hospital entrance. A young Asian man hopped out and opened the back door for her. He was wearing a jacket that reminded Megan of a sea captain.

"You are Ms. Megan Mully?" he asked.

"Yes," she replied.

"I'm Jeffrey Wong, Mr. Wake's driver. I'll be delivering you to your interview this afternoon."

For half a second, she wondered if she needed to tip the man. She wasn't used to being driven around by a chauffeur. But then, if he worked for a wealthy gentleman, she shouldn't have to worry about that sort of thing. She climbed into the limo and sat facing forward. Her purse had its own personal space on the roomy seat.

Wong leaned in to point out amenities. "If you'd like a refreshment, there's a mini fridge. It will take us about half an hour to reach our destination. Please, make yourself comfortable."

The door closed and Megan leaned back on the seat and exhaled with a whoosh. She wanted to get it out of her system before the driver got back in the car. She still had the newspaper with the ad in it, and she folded it tightly and clutched it in her lap for the first five minutes.

After that, she relaxed a bit and explored the mini fridge. She wasn't hungry. More curious than anything. Even so, she couldn't resist trying one of the little sandwiches on a tray. And a girl could never have enough caffeine. She popped the top on another soda, a diet drink this time. The fruit looked appealing, too, especially since she had no idea where she would be at dinner time or if she could afford to spend any of her forty dollars on a real meal. Very carefully, she smuggled an apple and a banana into her purse for later.

Megan wondered how many applicants had already ridden to their interview in the limo. If the offer was legit, she feared she would not have any of the necessary skills. What did a personal secretary do, anyway? In the age of iPhones and computers and email, did people even use secretaries anymore? The ones she'd known in the college departments all had different titles. They were office managers or clerical assistants or IT techs. Not a single one ever said she or he was a secretary.

For a few minutes, she looked out the window, but the glass was heavily tinted, and she didn't really know what the streets were. Nothing looked familiar. She had the strangest feeling that she'd woken up from a long ugly dream and now she was emerging into a new world.

A twinge of panic rattled her insides. Her mouth dried up and she clutched her newspaper tighter, while she sipped at her soda.

Nothing bad will happen, she thought. *For all they know, I've relayed my destination to my mother who might be a senator or a policewoman or a mob wife. They can't possibly know. They won't try anything shady.*

Having calmed herself sufficiently, she tried breathing normally and found that air would still slide in and out of her lungs.

Sooner than she expected, the limo pulled into a parking garage beneath an office building. In one fell swoop, they left the sunlight and dove down into the dark maw of commerce. Megan already missed the sun.

Chapter Three

KEVIN PACED THE LENGTH of the rented office. He glanced at the art on the walls. It wasn't exactly what he would have chosen, but he was forced to take some short cuts. Time was of the essence. The wedding was six days away and he still had no bride.

He'd already interviewed twenty-seven women for the gentleman's secretary position, and turned away a young gay man who came prepared to convince him that what he really needed was a male secretary. The women so far this week had been a mixed bag of disappointment. One of them was in her forties. Two of them were thirtyish, trying to pretend they were twenty-five. He took their resumes and promised to give them a decision by the end of the week. He didn't even tell them what the job was really all about. The other four women were the right age, but one had a snarky, hostile manner and a grating laugh. His family would never believe that Kevin was madly in love with her. She chewed gum and her skirt was too short. Another was too tall. That was hard to do, since Kevin was six four. He stood in the middle of the room and looked up at her in amazement for several seconds before rushing through an interview that he already knew was pointless.

The remaining two women had been possibles. He had gone so far as to explain in part what the job actually entailed, acting the part of his fiancée. He did not tell them why. He didn't get a chance to. The first one got up in the middle of his explanation and left without a word. The second told him she had a good mind to report him for soliciting.

16

It never occurred to him that such an issue would arise. He was adamant that no sex was involved or requested. He just wanted to get engaged and married before his twenty-fifth birthday.

The phone on the desk rang softly. Everything in the room whispered elegance and money, from the thick carpet to the rich mahogany of the desk and the leather of the chairs. The phones in here didn't jangle, they gently drew your attention to an incoming call. Kevin liked that a lot, and he hoped it would be impressive enough to convince the right woman that he already had the riches he was hoping to inherit on June 30.

"Yes?"

The chauffeur's voice announced, "She's on her way up in the private elevator."

"Thank you."

Kevin hung up and opened the double doors that separated the posh office from the private elevator on the other side of the well appointed waiting room. Another smaller mahogany desk sat against one wall. It held a computer and a phone, nothing else.

The elevator doors pinged open.

The woman inside was young with ash blond hair that fell below her shoulders. Her sky blue eyes were startling in their intensity. She was five eleven, very lean, and a bit pale. She looked oddly out of place in her summer dress and flats. He found himself imagining a bathing suit beneath the frock, leaving those long, lean legs bare. She was so lovely, his composure was momentarily rattled. He shook off the thoughts about her legs and greeted her.

"Ms. Megan Mully?"

Megan stepped out of the elevator, purse over one arm, newspaper under the other. She extended a hand.

"Mr. Kevin Fineman Wake?"

"In person. Won't you come into my office? I've given the receptionist the day off." He stood aside and let her enter the large room. The tall windows and the view of the city was impressive. He wanted to make the most of it.

Megan tried to look everywhere at once. She'd been in a big office before, but only on church business with her parents. She'd never seen this kind of opulence. She decided it looked nice enough, but it needed a work table. The large polished desk was no place to spread papers and sharpen pencils.

"Do you actually work in here?" The question just popped out. She tried to cover her eruption of personal opinion by adding, "The view must be distracting."

Kevin straightened his new suit jacket and replied, "When I'm working, I don't even notice the view. Won't you sit down? Would you like a coffee?"

"No, thank you. I had something in the limo." Megan suppressed a giggle. "Sorry. I have never in my life had occasion to say anything like that before."

Kevin smiled. "No problem. Shall we talk about the position?"

Megan sat on the deep leather chair in front of the desk, set her purse on the floor and lay the newspaper on top of it. "Oh, yes, please. I have a hundred questions."

Kevin sat down behind the desk and steepled his fingers. "How old are you?"

"Twenty-four."

"Do you know how to use a word processing program? Are you computer literate?"

"I have a Bachelor's degree in social work," said Megan. "I am definitely literate."

"Work history? Resume?"

"Oh, I'm sorry, I just saw your ad this morning, and I wasn't near my computer." No, her computer was lying in a jumbled mess somewhere in the trunk of her wrecked car, probably in a junkyard being sold for parts. "So I just called and came. I could bring you one tomorrow."

Kevin waved it away. "That may not be necessary. Are you discreet?"

Megan took a moment to think.

"It's a simple question," said Kevin.

"But not a simple answer," she replied. "No one has ever asked me that before. I'm examining myself."

Kevin covered his mouth to hide a grin. If nothing else, she was entertaining.

"Well?" he prompted after several seconds passed.

"Yes," said Megan. "I believe I am."

"Do you have any life-threatening allergies?"

"None that I know of." Curiouser and curiouser. What did a person's allergies have to do with being a personal secretary?

"Do you like dogs?"

"Oh, yes." Maybe it was work environment related.

"Cats?"

"They have a purpose in life."

"Horses?"

"Noble animals."

"That's not an answer."

"The word 'horses' by itself is not a question. Is it my turn?"

Kevin smiled and leaned back in his chair. "By all means."

Megan straightened her spine and folded her hands in her lap. "Is your last name Wake, or is it Fineman Wake?"

"Legally, Wake. Fineman is my mother's family, so I carry that name as well."

"Your ad says 'willing to relocate.' Do you have a single destination in mind, or does it involve extensive travel?" She didn't want to face the exhaustion of airports, long flights, and tourism so soon after her hospital stay.

"One location, maybe two at most. Whoever gets the job will be coming to Colorado with me right away."

Megan brightened. "I was born in Colorado."

Kevin slumped and frowned. He couldn't afford for his pretend bride to know all about the Finemans and the family fortunes. Granted, he was going to pay her for a role, but he didn't necessarily want someone with extended foreknowledge of just how rich his family was.

Megan rushed on. "But if that's a deal breaker, I can pretend I was born elsewhere."

Kevin's frown evaporated. "Where did you grow up?"

"Mostly in California. My dad is a minister, and he kept moving from town to town, looking for a church that needed him."

"Do your parents live here?" Kevin hoped she hadn't said anything to them yet. But then, all they would know would be that she was applying for a job as personal secretary. Nothing to worry about.

"No, they're in Guatemala. That's where dad finally found a church. A mission, actually."

The frown was back. "You said you had to give your mother this address."

Megan blushed. She rolled her eyes. "Of course, silly. In case you were a serial killer. Someone had to know where I was."

"So you called Guatemala?"

"I was planning to eventually."

Kevin laughed. He cut it short and grew serious again. "Look, Megan, I think you have a real chance at this job. There are some aspects of it that I need to explain before you make your final decision. Are you an open-minded person?"

"That depends. If you are the head of a secret cult, then no, I'm probably not open-minded enough for you. If you're a legitimate employer, then yes, I may fit the bill."

"Oh, this is a legitimate offer of employment. But the duties may vary a bit from what most people consider appropriate for a personal secretary."

This time it was Megan who slumped in her chair. "Please don't tell me you're just looking for a date or a masseuse."

"No, that's not it at all." Kevin liked Megan more and more, every time she opened her mouth. She was funny and direct and fresh. She was perfect. Now if only he could convince her to take the job.

"There's nothing sexual or inappropriate involved in this position at all. It's just not exactly a secretarial position in the traditional sense. You see, I need someone who can listen when I talk and retain information about my family and my business interests. I need someone who can comport themselves with dignity and composure in social situations. I need someone who doesn't hate small boys."

It was Megan's turn to laugh. "That's a good one. Fairly specific, too."

Kevin offered a crooked smile. "I have a little brother."

"What else do you need?" Megan was enjoying the way his face shifted from sternly serious to truly amused. When he was stern he looked like he might be thirty-something, but when he smiled, she guessed his age to be close to hers. And when he laughed, he looked like a little boy. It was an attractive mix.

Kevin hesitated. Twice he'd gotten this far, and twice the candidates had stomped out in fury. He chose his words carefully. He did not want Megan to hurl epithets and flee.

"I have a complicated family situation," he began. "My parents are *not* in Guatemala. They are very much here in the States. And there is a hundred-year-old legal arrangement governing my inheritance. I need your help to guarantee that I meet those legal requirements. In exchange, I will pay you handsomely, cover all housing and transportation, and when everything is secure, there will be a large bonus in it for you."

Megan tilted her head to one side and narrowed her gaze. "Are you sure there's no sex involved?"

"I've had a legal contract drawn up for you examine, if we get that far. The no sex part is written into the contract. You will not be forced or coerced to do anything you do not want to do."

"You were right. It's not what I would expect from a job as personal secretary." She tilted her head to the other side. "On the other hand, if you have lawyers involved, the chances of you being a serial killer are much reduced. They tend to work alone."

Kevin smiled again. "We seem to have a rapport," he said. "That is encouraging."

Megan shook a finger back and forth in the air and said, "We have repartee," she said. "That's not quite rapport."

"But it's a beginning. Is it enough to do business together?"

Megan's brows knit together and she leaned forward, hands clasped. "Let me see if I understand you. You want me to learn a ton of stuff about your family, then deal with your parents and your kid brother."

"I have a teenage sister, too. Do you know much about teenage girls?"

"I spent several years as one," said Megan. "My advice to your sister is to age as quickly as possible."

Kevin nodded and replied in a serious tone, "I'll pass that on to her."

"You also want me to help you jump through legal hoops so you can receive your inheritance."

"Correct."

"I'm not a lawyer," said Megan. "I have no background whatsoever in law."

"Not necessary."

"Then how on earth could I help you with legal rigamarole?"

Kevin took a deep breath and let it out slowly. His fingers drummed the surface of the desk. "I need to be legally married before my twenty-fifth birthday."

Megan blinked at him. "You want me to plan your wedding?"

"Not exactly."

Megan leaned back in her chair and pinned Kevin with a sideways glance. "Just what *do* you want me to do?"

Kevin braced himself for another fiery exit, then said flat out, "I need you to agree to marry me until my inheritance is secured. Once that happens, and a decent amount of time passes, we can arrange a discreet divorce. You will receive a handsome settlement, and I will have control of what is rightfully mine."

Megan sat quietly for several seconds. Then she stood up and slung her purse over her shoulder.

Kevin thought, *Here it comes. She's going to stomp out, just like the others.*

But instead, Megan asked, "May I use your restroom?"

"Oh. Of course. It's that door by the Picasso."

Megan retreated to the bathroom.

Kevin plopped backward in his chair and closed his eyes for a moment. At least she hadn't walked out. Yet.

He waited five minutes. Seven. Ten.

He got up and began to pace. Then he stopped and stared out the windows. Megan was right. How could anyone get any real work done in here with that view beckoning?

A soft click behind him announced Megan's return. He whirled in time to see her take her seat. She was holding a paper towel on which she had written some notes.

Megan cleared her throat. "First of all, that is a Picasso print, not an original. I'm sure you know that, but I just wanted you to know that I do, too."

Kevin nodded. "Okay."

"As I said before, I know nothing about the law, but isn't it illegal to marry someone for personal gain?"

Kevin shrugged. "No. If you want to get nit-picky, women do it all the time. Not every couple marries for love."

Megan bobbed her head once to acknowledge that fact. "But I remember in college, a girl got in a ton of trouble for agreeing to marry a Russian engineering student so he could stay in the country and get a green card."

Kevin spread his hands. "I'm not a foreign national. I'm an American citizen. As such, I have the right to get married if I want to. Correct?"

Megan bobbed her head again, then moved on to her next note. "You had a lawyer draw up the contract. Will I be allowed to show it to another lawyer? May I take a copy of it with me?"

Kevin squirmed.

Megan's head dropped. "So it *is* a trick, then."

"No, no, it's legit. I just can't let you take a copy away with you. You see, if my father's legal team sees this contract, I'm screwed."

"What if they see it after the wedding?"

22

Kevin's heart pounded. Could she be about to say yes to the arrangement? He was flustered and had to think before he answered.

"If they *ever* see this contract, they will raise hell in the courts for years."

"Then aren't you taking a terrible chance by showing this contract to anyone? Even prospective signers?" Megan could see that he hadn't thought of that as his face fell and his brow furrowed with worry.

"I, er, didn't think of that."

"Did you show it to the other applicants?"

"No. We didn't get that far."

"And you haven't shown it to me yet, so you're safe."

"It includes a confidentiality clause."

Megan turned a hand over. "But that only helps if I actually sign the contract, right?"

"Oh, God, I'm screwed." Kevin slumped in the chair. Why hadn't he thought through to this point? Thank goodness he hadn't shown those other women the contract.

Megan smiled genuinely for the first time since she entered the room. He was definitely fallible and obviously in trouble.

But then, so was she. The dreaded envelope practically burned a hole in her purse.

Megan rose and pulled her chair up to the mahogany desk. She laid her paper towel notes out flat, then pulled the envelope out of her purse and set it in front of Kevin.

"I think we can help each other."

Chapter Four

"WHAT WE NEED," SAID MEGAN, "is a prenup. Your father's lawyers can never fault you for having a prenup, can they?"

"You mean, you'll do it? You'll pretend to be my bride?"

"Oh, don't be silly. I'm not pretending anything. If you want me to help you secure your inheritance, I can do that. But I need to know that you will keep your part of the bargain. So we will get married legally with a prenup." She tapped her finger on the envelope. "No matter what happens to our marriage, I need to know that this will be taken care of, either as your wife, or as part of the divorce settlement."

Kevin studied the envelope. The return address was a hospital imprint. He frowned as he pulled the papers out. Page after page of medical billing stared up at him.

"Yours?"

Megan nodded. "Car accident. Everything I owned was in that car. I was moving to the city to start a new job. Never made it. I've been in the hospital for six months."

Kevin couldn't stop himself from staring at her. "Sorry, but you look great. Perfectly normal."

"I am, now," she said. "My mother flew home from Guatemala and stayed with me through the surgery and my first two weeks of physical therapy. But my father needed her at the mission. He's building a school for orphans down there. So when mother felt like I was going to be okay, she went back. She left me forty dollars in

24

cash and a mailing address for the mission. They're very dedicated people."

Kevin's brow darkened. "Pretty damn cold, if you ask me."

Megan tucked her chin. "Really? Not at all like your father, who wants to rip your inheritance out of your hands, right?"

Kevin held up an index finger. "You win that point."

"Can you do it?" asked Megan, nodding at the envelope. "Do you have that much money? Or is this all a scam to get a girl in bed?"

"It's not a scam."

"Good. Because there will be no sexual contact until or unless I say so. After all, rape is rape, even when people are married, and since we are conducting a business deal here and you need your father to believe we are deeply in love and legitimate, it would ruin everything if I had to report you for rape. Details about our meeting today might get out."

Kevin felt a cold knot form in his gut. He hadn't seen that coming. If he didn't pay her medical bills and legally marry her, she would go to his father. He hadn't realized how attractive he thought she was until she shattered his growing fondness for her.

But he couldn't show her the door. If she was willing to blatantly blackmail him, he didn't dare kick her out. Besides, this was what he wanted in the first place, right? He had to agree to her terms in order to secure his siblings' future.

She was a smart blackmailer, he had to give her that. She wanted a legal marriage and a prenup. Well, fine, he'd give her a prenup. He pulled himself together and turned the most businesslike face he could manage in her direction.

"All right,. Do you want that in the prenup? No sex against your will? Or is my word enough?"

Megan could feel him drawing back. She wasn't sure why. She was just trying to help him out of his dilemma while helping herself out of hers. Wasn't that what he wanted? A fake marriage to guarantee he would inherit?

She found herself irrationally irritated by his sudden cold shoulder. "You have to be a better actor than that if you want to pull this off. If we're supposed to be in love, you can't be distant." She tapped the envelope. "Can you do it?"

Kevin nodded. "It won't be a problem." He tried to ignore his disappointment and restore the easy banter they had shared earlier, but he couldn't think of anything witty to say. "You were right," he said sadly. "Repartee is not the same thing as rapport."

Megan found her resolve weakening. She put a hand to her mouth, searching for the right words. "You were ready to have me sign a contract," she said. "Now you're acting like my request for a prenup is all hard and cold. I don't understand. The legal safeguards are okay for you, but they're wrong when they're my idea?"

That hit Kevin between the eyes. He sat stunned for a moment.

"Fine," said Megan. "I knew it was too good to be true." She stuffed the medical bills back in the envelope and shoved everything into her purse. The fruit she'd taken from the limo got in the way. She dumped it on the desk. "This was supposed to be my dinner, but I don't want you to think I'm cheating you out of anything. So you keep this. It came from your mini fridge. Wish I could say it was nice meeting you." She stood up and headed for the door.

"Wait!" Kevin shot out of his chair and beat her to the door. He blocked her path, his hands up in surrender. "Please, don't leave."

Megan pulled up short and waited for an explanation.

Kevin spread his hands. "I didn't realize I was doing that," he said. "What you said. Wanting legal safeguards for me but not wanting any for you. I never looked at it that way. Please. Let's be businesslike. You need your medical bills paid, and I need your help."

Megan's shoulders loosened. "Okay, then. Let's make a list." She returned to her chair at the desk.

Kevin followed her. Whatever she had in mind, he could deal with it. He just had to get through that wedding and the transfer of the family trust into his hands. He would pay whatever price he had to pay to secure the future for his brother and sister. He didn't have to live with this arrangement forever.

Megan waited for him to sit before she asked, "When can we get this agreement written up? How soon will it take effect?"

Kevin grimaced. She was so eager to begin reaping the benefits. Then he caught himself again. Maybe she was right. Maybe he was applying a double standard. He would reap benefits, too, as soon as they got through the wedding. He cleared his throat to cover the grimace.

"I can deliver the details to the lawyer today and have him here tomorrow morning with papers for us to sign."

Megan seemed relieved. "Excellent. All right. Here's what I was thinking." She laid her notes out again on the desk.

Kevin leaned forward and studied her tidy handwriting. He read the list three times, then turned the paper towel over. Nothing there.

"This is it?"

Megan looked uncertain. "Is it too much?"

Kevin was confused. If she did turn out to be a blackmailer, she wasn't very good at the extortion part.

"Basically you are asking for me to pay off your medical bills?"

"Well, that and the $20,000 to cover the income I would have made if I'd been able to take my new job." Megan's features twisted. "And if I could have $200 of that in advance, I could get a hotel room for the night and maybe buy an outfit that wasn't picked off the Salvation Army racks."

Well, that explained why she looked so odd in her summer frock, thought Kevin. It didn't suit her because it was a charity dress, and when you have nothing to wear, you take what you can get.

That realization humbled him. Megan was taking him up on his job offer because she literally had nothing, not even a place to spend the night.

Kevin never wanted his sister Karla to be in that situation. He never wanted her to have to sell her dignity to pay a medical bill or wonder where she was going to sleep or what she was going to eat for dinner. This marriage of convenience wasn't convenient for anyone, not even for Megan.

Kevin pulled out his wallet and counted out a thousand in cash. "Here."

"But that's way too much," said Megan.

"We're going to be engaged and married, right? I had no idea you were living on the street. Take this and buy some clothes. Jeffrey, my chauffeur, will drive for you. I know it's just a stop gap measure, but be sure to include a pair of jeans and comfortable walking shoes. We'll be going to the family ranch for the wedding. When you're done shopping, Jeffrey will take you to the Hilton. I have a suite there, and you'll have your own room. Oh, take the fruit. You might get hungry while you're shopping."

Megan looked overwhelmed. "Thank you. And the prenup?"

"I'll be very busy this afternoon, getting those details taken care of, among others." He glanced at his watch. "You'd better go. It's already after three." He picked up the phone. A moment later, he spoke. "Jeffrey? Megan is coming down in the private elevator. She needs to shop for clothes this afternoon. Please put it on my credit card and see to her every need."

Chapter Five

MEGAN LET JEFFREY ESCORT her back to the limo. She was delighted to have a driver. She didn't think she trusted herself behind the wheel of a car since her accident. She'd had far too many nightmares in the hospital, revisiting the crash. Every time she dreamed about it, she realized how close she'd come to dying.

The thousand dollars in her purse made her feel a little better about the arrangement she was about to enter into. But she couldn't help being a little worried. Maybe scared was a better word. Even so, the sound of Kevin promising to pay off that onerous medical bill was music to her ears.

Of course, there was still the worry that he was a serial killer or had some other nefarious plans in mind. But Jeffrey Wong seemed like a stand-up guy. Oddly enough, she felt perfectly safe with Jeffrey. Maybe it was the uniform. Or maybe it was the gorgeous interior of the limousine. She helped herself to another soda and ate her banana during the drive to the mall. She decided she would call her mother before the end of the day. At least that way, someone, somewhere would know what she was doing. Just in case.

Jeffrey parked the limo, came to the door to let her out, then followed her into the mall.

"You can wait here, if you prefer," said Megan.

"Mr. Wake said I should see to your every need, ma'am. That would include carrying your bags and being ready with the credit card."

"Wow. Okay. I am definitely feeling pampered. I've never been in this mall before, but I'll try not to take too long." The truth was, she was feeling the fatigue of being out and about. She was missing the rest and relaxation of her hospital bed. She caught a glimpse of herself in the shop windows as she passed, and gasped in surprise.

"Is everything all right, ma'am?"

"Oh, fine. Sorry. I really do need to buy clothes, don't I?"

Jeffrey did not respond, but she could swear she saw the hint of a smile.

The frock they'd brought her from the donations closet fit her okay, but it was so different from anything she would have picked out for herself, she didn't even recognize the woman in the reflection. She was pale, and thinner than she had been six months before. She drew herself up and ignored the fatigue that hounded her. She needed clothes and fast!

Megan had no idea how much she would need, but if Kevin was willing to send her shopping with a thousand in cash and a chauffeur with a credit card, chances were good she would have an opportunity to add to her wardrobe later. So she concentrated on the basics. She allowed herself the luxury of purchasing top of the line items, instead of the WalMart bargains she'd been used to in college and afterward. She picked out all the necessities, and made sure she got two pairs of jeans. Then she indulged herself by draping blouses, tops, and summer suits over her arm to carry into the fitting room.

It took less than two hours to pick out more clothes than she'd ever bought in her life, and she still hadn't selected any outdoor wear, save the jeans. Kevin said they were going to a ranch. Well, she would just have to make do.

But one thing she knew for certain. She was not wearing the flowered frock out of the mall. She waved a saleslady into the dressing room.

"I just got out of the hospital," she said quietly. "I need to change and wear some of these clothes. Is that possible?"

The saleslady's eyes grew wide when she saw the collection of items in the changing room. "Oh, that will be fine. Pick out what you plan to change into and I'll keep the tags for you at the register. You can hand them to me over the door."

When Megan emerged from the dressing room, she was elegant in a form-fitting creamy linen jacket and slacks.

Jeffrey took the rest of her selections gently out of the saleslady's arms and followed her to the register.

"I'll pay for these, ma'am," he said, pulling out the credit card.

Megan looked down at her outfit approvingly, and felt one hundred percent better. Then she muttered, "Darn! I need shoes."

"No problem," said Jeffrey. "There are several shoe stores in this mall."

Laden with Megan's bags, Jeffrey followed her uncomplainingly through three shoe stores. When Megan hesitated over the purchase of hiking boots, Jeffrey quietly informed the salesperson, "Madame will also take the hiking boots."

Megan left with running shoes, hiking boots, a pair of chunky heels, white sandals, and tan and cream flats with a strap over the instep. She discarded the white canvas shoes from the charity closet and wore the flats out of the store, a perfect match for her linen suit.

"Jeffrey, I vote we head for the hotel," said Megan, refusing to let him carry all the shoe bags along with the clothes. "I'm tired and hungry."

By the time they returned to the limo, Megan practically collapsed onto the back seat. Jeffrey stored everything in the trunk, then got behind the wheel.

"Would you care for a snack on the way back to the hotel, ma'am? Or you can order from room service after you arrive."

"I'm almost too tired to eat," said Megan. "Let's go to the hotel." She let her head fall back on the car seat. She'd never been in such a comfortable vehicle before. She found herself fantasizing about turning it into a mobile apartment. It had a fridge. The seats were comfortable enough to sleep on. And Jeffrey could just spend his life driving her around.

She didn't realize she'd fallen asleep until Jeffrey touched her arm, gently calling her name.

"Ms. Mully? Ms. Mully, we're here. Let me escort you to the express elevator. Your suite is on the thirty-fifth floor. Mr. Wake is already there. I'll bring your bags up shortly."

Megan straightened up and gave him an apologetic look.

"Sorry. Guess I was more tired than I thought. What time is it?"

"Eight thirty, ma'am."

"Not too late for room service?"

Jeffrey looked amused. "It's never too late for room service when you travel with Mr. Wake."

"Oh." Megan felt like a fish out of water, but she was certain she could get used to this kind of life, given enough time. Say, another half an hour. "Great."

Jeffrey called the elevator for her and waited for the doors to close.

Too late, Megan realized she didn't have a room key. Oh, well, she'd just wait for him to come up with her things.

The elevator doors slid open silently and Megan stepped out into a private lobby. The double doors in front of her were slightly ajar. When she went through the doors, she was in a sitting room that extended fifty feet across. One wall was all glass and looked out over the city. The view of a million windows glimmering with the reflection of the setting sun was breathtaking.

Kevin straightened up from behind the bar, where he'd put ice in two glasses. When he saw Megan, his approval showed on his features.

"I like this outfit a lot better than the old one," he said. "Cold drink?"

"Iced tea?" asked Megan.

Kevin nodded. "We've got it all. I take it the shopping went well."

"Yes, thank you. Jeffrey will be up in a moment."

Kevin chuckled. "You're adjusting nicely. That sounded like something my mother would say."

Megan made a face. "I hope that's not a bad thing."

Kevin delivered her iced tea. "Shall I make you a list of phrases *not* to use?"

Megan sipped tea, and her eyes closed with delight. "Maybe that would be a good idea. Forgive me, but I need to sit down." Her free hand moved automatically to her right thigh. She moved to a bank of sofas and sank onto one, dropping her purse at her feet. For a moment she stared at it as if it were a bug that had crawled out from under the sofa.

"What is it?" asked Kevin.

Megan sighed. "I shopped for four hours and never even thought about getting a nice handbag."

Kevin shrugged. "There'll be plenty of time for that. Did you want to see my notes on the prenup?"

"Oh, please, not now," said Megan. "Jeffrey said I could order something to eat from room service. I need to eat and lie down. Today's schedule was a huge increase over my activity level in the hospital."

"Okay," said Kevin. "It's been a long day for me, too."

"If I'm still awake after I eat, I'll look at the notes."

"What would you like?"

"Is there a menu?"

"Somewhere, yes. But you don't need one. Just tell me what you want and I'll have it sent up."

"Wow. Nice." Megan stifled a yawn. On a whim, she said, "How about a bleu cheese burger and a salad? And if you don't mind, may I lie down for a few minutes while we wait for the food?"

"No problem. Your door is down that corridor. In case you still think I might be a serial killer, feel free to lodge a chair under the door knob so I can't get in." He kept a straight face while he said it.

"Thank you," said Megan. She got up and headed down the short hallway to the crimson and gilt double doors. "At least I'll die in splendor." Then she opened the double doors and quietly closed them behind her.

Chapter Six

KEVIN ORDERED DINNER. He was pleased that Megan hadn't taken his thousand dollars and bailed on Jeffrey. That was a good sign. But then again, if she was really planning to blackmail him, a measly thousand was just the tip of the iceberg.

On the other hand, she had looked adorable in her new linen suit. Her long blond hair was just the color he enjoyed. It would look perfect if she had a tan. But then she said she'd been in the hospital. Those pages of medical bills bore that out. So she wasn't a liar.

He stood for a long while, looking out over the city skyline. Night was falling slowly, as it did in the summertime. The sun was no longer visible but it still had the power to paint strokes of pink and orange on the underbellies of puffy clouds. But indigo was creeping in from the east, and it wouldn't be long before the city was a sparkling array of lights. *Like a giant Christmas tree slumbering on its side*, he thought.

"Very poetic," he said aloud. "Save your creativity for after your birthday."

He turned away from the long bank of windows and poured himself an iced tea from the tall pitcher on the bar. He pressed a toggle on the wall and soft music wafted from invisible speakers.

Jeffrey's voice startled him. "Pretty impressive setup." He dropped the shopping bags he had carried in on the carpet. They landed soundlessly.

"Oh, hey. I didn't hear you come in."

33

"Blame the carpeting. This place is amazing! When you offered me this gig, I had no idea what kind of operating budget you were talking about."

Kevin made a face. "My mother sends me money every month. She can't stand the idea of me actually having to survive on the wages I earn. I've been putting it in the bank. Trust me, I couldn't afford to live like this all year. Want some iced tea?"

Jeffrey went around to the service side of the bar. "Let me pour. You don't want your fiancée to see you treating me as an equal. When are you going to tell her the truth?"

Kevin stretched his neck from side to side, getting the kinks out. "I was going to do it tonight, but I don't know. A couple of things she said during our interview made me leery." He lowered his voice. "I can't shake the feeling that she already knows everything and she's planning to blackmail me."

Jeffrey's head bulleted back. "Are we talking about the same woman? The Megan I took shopping was very sweet and considerate and she was practically counting prices on her fingers, trying not to spend too much."

"Really?"

"Yes. I think you're being paranoid. But then again, maybe that comes with the territory. After all, you are trying to pull a fast one on your old man, and you are not the most devious person in the world."

"No, but he is. And that's what scares me. What if he already sniffed this whole thing out and planted her here? I wouldn't put it past him. What if she's one of his marionettes?"

"I picked her up in front of a hospital," said Jeffrey. "But I guess anyone could stand in front of a building and look lost and pitiful."

Kevin frowned. "Stop guilt-tripping me. I plan to keep my word, as long as she sees this thing through." He ran a hand over his mouth. "And those medical bills looked real enough. Of course, my old man wouldn't have any problem forging something like that."

Jeffrey took his chauffeur's cap off and set it on the bar. He used silver tongs to drop four cubes of sugar into his tea.

"There goes your paranoia again," he said. "I think even your father would have trouble seeing through the 'personal secretary' ruse. Your name wasn't on the ad, remember? You placed an ad and rented an office, and you called me and made me a part of this whole charade, for which I thank you very much, by the way. This pays way better than an entry level position with an engineering firm."

"You're welcome."

Jeffrey grinned. "I'm just saying, there was nothing for your father to pick up on, so Megan couldn't possibly be working for him."

"No, I guess not. But she could still be planning to blackmail me."

"You are an idiot," said Jeffrey lightly. He glanced around. "She in her room?"

Kevin nodded.

"Did my cousin take care of your prenuptial agreement?"

"Yes, thanks. He did a great job. Thank God for friends. I didn't know who to trust with the details. He's quite a bit older than you, isn't he?"

"Just ten years, but he looks older. That's why I went into engineering. Law is too stressful. He usually works with international importers and exporters, but he does other stuff, too. When his wife divorced him three years ago, he learned a whole lot about marital law in self-defense. Don't worry, he knows what he's doing. Is that the document?"

Kevin nodded and tapped a fingertip on three pages of small print laid out on the bar. "This is it. I hope she doesn't bail when she reads this."

"You put in the part about you being able to end the marriage at the appropriate time?"

"Yeah, but your cousin said she needs to be able to do the same or it'll look rigged and fake for sure. If my father ever sees these documents, it has to look like a real prenup or I'm screwed."

"This is so cool," said Jeffrey. "Tell me again how much money you inherit on your birthday."

Kevin punched Jeffrey playfully in the shoulder. "Way more than your puny brain could handle. Now shut up and answer the door. I ordered room service."

Jeffrey grinned on his way across the room. "Hey, man, for that kind of money, I'd wear a wig and falsies and marry you myself if I thought we could fool your father."

"Very funny," said Kevin. He strode across the room, glancing toward the doors of Megan's suite. He put a hand on Jeffrey's arm and said quietly, "If you value your paycheck, don't joke around like that again. She might have heard you."

Jeffrey grew serious. "Sorry, Kev. I'll stay in character."

Kevin nodded, then realized he was still holding onto Jeff's arm. He let go. "Thanks."

Jeffrey threw his shoulders back and held his nose an inch higher than usual as he opened the door.

"Room service?"

"Thank you," said Jeffrey, in character. "Right over there, please." He pulled five dollars out of his pocket and slipped it to the waiter.

"Thank *you*, sir." The waiter left happy.

Jeffrey allowed himself a tiny smile. "I really like doing that," he said. "Tipping and stuff. Especially with your money."

"Great. Don't get used to it yet. I've still got to get married."

"I'd better take her purchases down the hall. Shall I tell her that dinner has arrived?"

"Yes, thank you."

Jeffrey winked and whispered, "Very imperious. Good job. We both need to stay in character. Me as the underling and you as the mega rich overlord."

Kevin was taken aback. Had he fallen into his role that easily? After five years of earning a living like normal people? The thought horrified him. Once he secured his siblings' futures, maybe he could give his share to charity. But what if that wasn't enough? What if he was really his father's son after all?

That thought chilled him to the bone.

Chapter Seven

MEGAN COULDN'T PUT IT off any longer. She had to let her parents know that she was out of the hospital and doing well. If she didn't call, her mother would be heartbroken when she learned that Megan had gone on with her life without giving her an update. And her mother always found out.

Her dad? Well, he wouldn't care one way or another, and that was fine with Megan. They had said their goodbyes the day she decided to go to college instead of following her parents to Guatemala.

"Missionary work is important," he said. "More important than running around with your high school friends for another four years. It's time you settled down into some good works." His voice had shaken the walls of the flimsy rental they were living in.

Megan had found herself backed against a wall, her father's words banging against her eardrums and her sensibilities. But if she surrendered about college, she knew she would never see her friends again, and she would lose all hope of living her own life.

"Yell all you want, dad. I'm not going to Guatemala. I'm going to college. I have an acceptance letter!"

"Well, I'm not paying for it! I'm not going to pay someone to turn my daughter away from the path of the Holy toward the worldly! And I'm not yelling, I'm voicing my opinion!"

Vernon Mully's features always looked angry, even when he professed to be happy about something. Megan had a theory. She thought all those years of preaching the wrath of God had soured his visage to the point that he could no longer smile or look happy.

Glenda Mully stepped in quietly, as she always did. "Vernon, a stranger would think you're threatening our daughter if he saw you looking so intent. Why don't you back away. Megan, you come stand over here. There are lots of people of faith out in the world. There's even a campus ministry. I've been reading Megan's brochures. And she *is* going to college."

"There's no money for college," bellowed Vernon.

"Megan knows that. She plans to work her way through, don't you, dear."

"Yes," said Megan. "I've always known I'd have to pay for it myself."

"Well, go, then," said Vernon, his volume inching down a bit. "If college is what you want, just go. We'll build the mission ourselves! I have to work on my sermon." And with that, slightly deflated, he left them alone.

"Your father—"

"I know, I know," said Megan. "He means well. He always means well. He just thinks God can't love anybody who doesn't bluster and yell all the time."

"His powers of persuasion used to be more subtle, when we were younger."

"Oh, mom, do you have to go to Guatemala? Isn't there good work he could do here in the States?"

Glenda Mully pushed a stray lock of hair out of Megan's face. "I've followed him everywhere else," she said, "like a dutiful wife, and I guess I'll follow him to Guatemala. But don't you worry. You'll hardly know I'm gone. You'll be at school, meeting new people, learning wonderful things! I'm so proud of you." She lowered her voice. "And there's something I want to show you. Come with me."

She led Megan into the tiny bedroom that Megan had decorated by covering the walls with pictures from magazines. Beautiful homes, new cars, even dogs and cats and ponies, were all lined up to represent the future she wanted for herself. A future that would never be hers if she ended up in Guatemala taking care of orphans with her parents.

"Close the door, dear."

Megan did so. She was puzzled, but she waited patiently while her mother pulled a box off the shelf of her closet. It was tucked far back from the edge, and Megan had never noticed it there.

"I always keep this in your room," said her mother softly, "because your father never comes in here."

Glenda settled on the edge of the narrow bed with the box in her lap. Her hands were roughened with work and her blond hair lightened with streaks of white and gray, but her blue eyes sparkled with the joy of her secret. She patted the bed and Megan sat beside her.

"What is it, mom?"

"Something I've been working on for years. It's our secret. If your father knew about it—" She paused. "—well, he doesn't, so let's keep it that way." She opened the box.

At first Megan thought it was empty. There was nothing inside. Nothing, except a small blue checkbook and a bank statement.

"I've been saving a little here and there over the years," said Glenda. "When I saw that spark of learning in you, that joy you expressed every morning on your way out the door to go to school, I knew I had to find a way to help you go to college. I know it's not much, but there's hardly any left over after running the household, you know."

Megan unfolded the bank statement and her mouth dropped open. "Mama! There's five thousand dollars in here!"

"Shhh. The Guatemalan mission attracts donors. Your father has already raised seventy thousand toward the building. This money here came from me scraping and doing without for years. And I didn't do all of that to buy windows and doors for strangers. It's not much as far as college expenses go, but it will get you a room near campus. It'll go quite a ways if you're careful."

Megan hugged her mother tight. "Oh, I will be. I'll be so careful, mom! And I'll get a job right away, and I'm a resident here so I don't have to pay out-of-state tuition." Her voice caught in her throat. "Thank you, mama."

Glenda smiled. "And as for me being in Guatemala, just remember our code word."

Megan wiped a tear away. "Code word?"

"At camp that year, remember? Your father's parishioners wanted the church to sponsor a summer camp experience? And you didn't want to go because you were only eight and the other kids were ten or older?"

Megan nodded. Her lips formed a grim line. "And dad said it would look bad if his child didn't attend because he was the pastor. I was scared to death."

"You'd never been away from home before," said her mother. "I tried to convince your friends' parents to exchange sleepovers, but your little friends were afraid of your father."

"He's blustery," said Megan.

Her mother laughed. "Yes, he is. So when you packed for camp, what did I tell you?"

"When you called me every night to see if I was okay, all I had to do was say the secret code word and you would come get me, no matter what."

"That's right. You never had to use it, though, because when you got to camp, you had so much fun."

Megan nodded. "I did, didn't I?" She didn't add that a big part of her fun was the fact that her father had not been around at camp to put his stern kibosh on everything she did. Megan put a finger to her lips and whispered, "Unicorn."

Glenda nodded. "That's right. You remembered."

Surrounded now by the luxury of Kevin Wake's hotel suite, Megan shook off the past and the tender feelings that crept up on her whenever she thought about her mother. She *had* remembered that code word. In the hospital after the accident, when the doctors told her she would need surgery and physical therapy, she asked a nurse to call her mother with a message: her location and the word "unicorn." And her mother came.

Megan was still on heavy pain medications when her mother had to leave again, so she couldn't recall if she ever found out how her mother got to her bedside from Guatemala. All she knew was that, when she came out of three days of induced coma, her mother was at her side.

Yes, she would have to call her mother and let her know that she was out of the hospital and doing well.

Physically, anyway. She reached for the hotel phone.

As for the rest of it?

She pulled her hand back. How would she explain the rest of it?

A soft knock at the door momentarily postponed that decision.

Chapter Eight

JEFFREY KNOCKED AGAIN. "Ms. Mully? Your dinner is here."

A moment later, Megan opened the door.

Jeffrey added, "I also brought your shopping bags up, ma'am." He waved a hand at the pile of purchases he'd set beside her door.

"Oh, thank you. I'll put them away." She reached for the bags.

"Your dinner will get cold," said Jeffrey. "I'll just set them inside the door for you. Mr. Wake is waiting."

"Oh, all right." Megan took a breath and headed for the living area with the wall of windows. She hadn't expected dinner to arrive so soon. The rest period she'd been craving had only lasted half an hour, but on the other hand she was famished.

Kevin Wake was seated at a table for two. His square jaw, piercing hazel eyes, and dark wavy hair made him look like a movie star, and the lavish surroundings only enhanced the feel of movie magic. Megan could imagine him tramping up and down hills with a lumberjack's axe on his shoulder. And she could equally picture him in a tuxedo at a Hollywood premiere. She pulled herself up short when she began to imagine him as a scantily clad lifeguard on a beach.

On closer inspection, Megan noticed that the table had wheels and realized this was how the waiter had delivered dinner.

"That was fast," she said.

Kevin indicated the other chair. "The service here has been excellent."

Megan sat and examined her plate. The bleu cheese burger and salad she'd requested awaited her. "Oh, this looks wonderful!"

Kevin suppressed a smile. "I love it when women enjoy their food."

Megan took her first bite and her eyes rolled in ecstasy. Around a mouthful of burger she mumbled, "Wommmberful."

Kevin laughed. "Good. I hope mine is that delicious." He cut into his steak.

Jeffrey cleared his throat.

"Yes, Jeffrey?"

"If you don't need me, sir, I'll retire for the evening."

"Certainly. Thanks for your help today."

Megan dabbed at her lips with her serviette. "Mmmm, yes, Jeffrey, thank you so much. I could not have handled all that shopping without you."

Jeffrey smiled at her. "You're welcome." He gave her a brisk nod and retreated to an area at the back of the suite.

Megan looked puzzled. "Where is Jeffrey's dinner?"

"In his room."

"But shouldn't he eat out here with us?"

Kevin sipped at a glass of wine. "That's not how it works," he said. "Servants do not eat with the family."

"Oh." Megan concentrated on her plate. She was glad this marriage thing was just a job, because she wasn't sure she could ever really marry a man who maintained such rigid class distinctions. Her disapproval floated in the air.

Kevin sighed. "Look, Megan, you will be going to the summer place in preparation for our wedding. It's important that you know how things work. Jeffrey and I have shared many meals together. But when it comes to my parents and the way they live, don't be shocked when you see the servants retiring to another room for meals. Except for when they're serving, of course."

"Of course." Megan tried to say it with a straight face, but she couldn't. She burst out laughing. "Sorry. This will take some getting used to."

After a while, Kevin said, "You never told me why you were in the hospital for so long. Even with serious injuries, don't they shove people out the front door as soon as they can?"

"Is it important?"

"Well, actually, it's a great cover story for why I haven't brought you to meet the parents sooner. I thought we could just go with the hospital thing as a reason why they don't know anything about you yet."

"That makes sense," said Megan. "The fewer lies we have to tell, the simpler this will be. I told you I was in a car accident. My injuries were serious and required surgery. The worst was a broken femur. It got infected, and I was on intravenous antibiotics for a very long time. Every time they thought we'd beat the infection and they took me off the IV, the darn thing would recur. I don't know if it was the same one or different every time. It didn't matter. They couldn't release me until that was cleared up. I would begin my physical therapy, then be so weakened by the infections that we had to start over."

"Sounds awful."

"It was. But the staff was very kind to me. Nurses are God's angels on earth. I don't think I would have survived it all if they hadn't been so kind."

Kevin lifted the lid on another large platter on the table. "Care for dessert?"

Megan's eyes lit up. "Is that bowl filled with whipped cream?"

"I like to spoon it on my chocolate cake," said Kevin. "Or perhaps you would prefer the Napoleon? Or the sorbet? Or the mousse?"

"Is the Napoleon that pastry that looks like it's wearing a uniform?"

"I never thought of it that way, but the icing does look a bit formal, doesn't it? Here." He handed her the plate with the Napoleon on it.

"And whipped cream," said Megan. "Pretty please."

Kevin smiled and spooned a large dollop of whipped cream on the pastry. "More?"

"Just a smidge more. Oh, a bigger smidge."

Kevin laughed and handed her the spoon. "Help yourself. Coffee?"

"Is it decaf? I need to sleep tonight."

"Decaf it is."

"Then definitely, coffee." Megan smiled back at him. Maybe this job wouldn't be too terrible after all. "So the whole ad in the paper for a personal assistant was just to meet women who might fit the bill as a fiancée?"

"That's right."

"I take it I fill it, since I'm here and you had the prenup papers drawn up."

"Oh, yes, the job is yours." His earlier doubts returned and he cleared his throat. "I suppose if I needed to verify that you spent the last six months in the hospital, I would be able to do that?"

"For a man looking for a woman desperate enough to pretend to be your wife, you seem quite suspicious. But yes, if you like, we can drop in on the staff at the hospital tomorrow and I'll introduce you all around. Feel better?"

Kevin settled back in his chair. "Yes, actually, I do."

Megan leaned across the table and stared into his eyes. "Do I look that deceitful?"

"You do not look deceitful at all, but then again, the best deceivers never look deceitful."

Megan gave a little moue. "Good point." She hummed with delight around another mouthful of dessert. "Mmmmm, this is so delicious."

Kevin wagged his brows at her. "There are a couple more selections here if you'd like to try them."

Megan held up a hand. "This is the richest and most delicious food I've had in months. Maybe ever. Hospital food earns its reputation for bland pap, you know. But I couldn't eat another bite."

Kevin drained his coffee cup. "In that case, would you feel up to reading the prenup?"

"Straight to business," said Megan. "I like that. Where is it?"

"On the bar. I had the lawyer keep it to three pages."

Megan rose and perched on a leather stool at the bar. She read silently through the document. Then she picked up a pen and began to make notes on a cocktail napkin.

Kevin watched her and let his mind wander. There was an old wives' tale that said women who enjoyed their food the way Megan did also enjoyed other activities with equal relish. He was wondering if that might be the case with her. She was certainly easy on the eyes, even in a state of fatigue. The linen suit she was wearing emphasized her long lean legs. The sound of her voice shattered his reverie.

"This document is totally unacceptable!"

Chapter Nine

IN THREE STRIDES, Kevin was beside her. "What's the problem? My lawyer and I worked for hours this afternoon getting this ready."

"But there is no mention of your promise to pay my medical bills!"

"As your husband, I would naturally do that."

"So you say now. But after we're among your family? And they remind you that these were bills incurred before we married? I'm sorry, I know I'm being paranoid, but the weight of this debt is crippling to me. I worked my way through college. I even worked two jobs at a time so I wouldn't have to take out loans. I took an extra year to finish because of my work schedule. And then just as I was about to start my new life, this accident wiped out everything I owned and took me out of the running for the new job I had lined up. All my hard work, for nothing. I've been shoved into a pit of debt through no fault of my own." Her voice broke.

Kevin grabbed a cocktail napkin and dabbed at her eyes. "Hey, hey, no need for tears. I'm a man of my word. This really worries you, doesn't it?"

Megan snuffled into the napkin and wiped the saltwater off her face. "I know to a rich man like you, this is no big deal. But for working stiffs like me and my parents, it feels like the end of the world. I haven't even started my life and I'm burdened with this huge obligation! My car insurance paid out to its limit, but those blasted infections wouldn't go away."

"There is always bankruptcy."

Megan's eyes flashed with fire. "Oh, really? Just like that? Marry me, Megan, to help me inherit my fortune, and when I don't need you any more, you can crawl away and declare bankruptcy and have that haunt your future credit line for seven years? No, thank you!"

Kevin was taken aback. "Seven years?"

"Yes! The hospital billing office started calling me for money three months ago. They dialed my hospital room number and told me they were taking me to collections because I hadn't paid anything on my bills yet. The floor nurse had to get on the phone and raise a ruckus and tell them to leave me alone at least until I was discharged."

The tears threatened to start again, but Kevin slipped an arm around her shoulders.

"Let's write an addendum," he offered. "Let's do it right now. You start. Here, let me get you some paper." He retrieved his briefcase and popped it open. Out came pens and a legal pad. "I'll call my lawyer and let him know we'll be faxing some changes tonight."

Megan's color was better now, although her hand shook as she pressed pen to paper.

"By the way, I should put your cell phone number in my phone," said Kevin.

"Don't have one anymore. Destroyed in the crash, and I didn't have an income to pay the bills anyway."

"Wow. Okay, that's on our list of things to do. Get you a new phone." He moved away to the windows to place his call.

A moment later, he was once again at Megan's side. "He hadn't even left for the day yet. Remind me to never become a lawyer."

Megan rewarded him with a muted laugh. "Here's what I have so far. What do you think?"

Kevin read her addition and nodded. "That should do it. A tidy promise to cover pre-existing medical bills. Let's both initial it. That's what Patrick said we should do if we're faxing it. Then he'll come by in the morning with the final version and we can sign it for real." He noticed she had written a separate paragraph on another sheet of paper. "What's this?"

Megan said, "I was hoping it would be all right if I included a weekly allowance for myself. I hate not having pocket money."

"You just put down $1,000. Don't you mean, one thousand a week?"

Megan looked horrified. "No! I was thinking of the thousand you already gave me. It turns out Jeffrey used your credit card for everything, so I still have that money in my bag. If we call it an allowance, I'll have cash and I won't feel so broke or dependent."

Kevin looked grim. "That is ridiculous. You—"

"Fine," snapped Megan. She was so tired, she couldn't take anymore. "I knew this whole thing was too good to be true." She slipped off the stool and went to retrieve her purse. Vibrating with fatigue, she pulled out the money and slapped it on the counter. "Here. And here's forty toward the linen suit I'm wearing. You'll have to wait for the rest on the suit because I need something to wear to job interviews."

Kevin grabbed her wrist, then immediately loosened his grip when she winced. "Would you wait just a second? Hear me out!"

Megan stood staring at his hand clamped around her wrist. Since she couldn't flee without cutting her arm off at the elbow, she took a calming breath and said, "I'm listening."

"I was about to say, a thousand dollars is ridiculous. You should get at least that much every week. In fact, you should get at least what I pay my chauffeur." He jotted a number on a napkin.

Megan's eyes grew wide. "Really?"

Kevin let go of her wrist. He knew he was probably just fueling her blackmail fires, but she was so convincing about not wanting to feel broke and dependent. He hated that feeling. More than once during the years he'd been away from his family, he'd wanted to dig into his allowance money. Now that he had to use that money to secure his future from his father's greed, he was feeling generous.

"How do you want it? Check? Cash? Direct deposit to a bank account?"

"I closed out my old one before my move. I don't have one at the moment."

"Not a problem. We'll deal in cash for the time being. Now put your partial payment back in your purse. Anything else we should add or delete from this document?"

Megan shook her head, feeling a bit sheepish after leaping to a wrong conclusion. "No. The rest seems okay."

"Fine. I'll fax this to Patrick."

Megan drooped with exhaustion.

"If we're all done, I really need to lie down," she said. "Are we traveling tomorrow or will we be staying here another night?"

Kevin tilted his head back and checked the ceiling as if his personal calendar were up there. "Let's see. Lawyer, safe deposit box at the bank..."

"On a Sunday?"

Kevin shrugged. "Why not? I arranged for the bank president to meet us there. It helps that he's a personal friend of my mother's. She helped him get his position, in fact. Is that such an unusual favor?"

Megan's brows shot skyward. "Not for the rich, I guess. What else is on the agenda?"

"That should do it." Mentally, he added, *Hospital, just to make sure you don't work for my father.* "And today is the twenty-third?" He shook his head in frustration. "We may have to stay here another day."

Megan's mood brightened. "Okay by me. Good night. Oh, what time do you need me in the morning?"

"I'm not sure. I was expecting Patrick around ten a.m."

"All right, then." She picked up her purse with her thousand dollar installment and headed down the hall to her room. She didn't know if she could trust Kevin or not. But for the moment, she couldn't think of any options.

The rich really are different, she thought. *How nice it must be to throw money around like that!*

Chapter Ten

Sunday, June 24

MEGAN WOKE UP WITH A START. She lay still, wondering what woke her. She looked at the clock by the bed. The digital readout said five thirty. Where was the nurse with her medication?

Then she remembered. She wasn't in the hospital anymore. She was lying in a very comfortable bed in a luxury suite at a posh hotel, and she was about to hire on as a bride for Kevin Wake, member of the one per cent.

Well, she bought that newspaper because she needed a job. And now she would have one. As soon as the prenup was signed.

But a prenup was just a piece of paper without a marriage. Without that, she didn't have anything. Not even a job.

That thought destroyed any hope of falling back to sleep. She threw off the covers and headed for the shower.

She picked out a pair of pastel blue capris and a matching sleeveless top. She'd chosen them because the color made her eyes even bluer, and because shorts were out of the question because of the scar on her leg. It was too fresh and she was too sensitive about it to hazard the stares she might get. Sport socks and white running shoes made her feel almost normal. She stood in the middle of the room and looked around.

She forced herself not to make the bed. That's what the hotel hired maids for.

That thought made her feel deliciously naughty. Then she laughed at herself as she went ahead and made it anyway.

She'd been too tired the night before to pull her purchases out of their bags. She set about doing that, knowing she would have to pack them up again soon. She got everything put away in the closet and the drawers, and once again she was standing in the middle of the room, looking around. It was only six thirty in the morning, and the lawyer wouldn't come until ten.

All of a sudden, she felt giddy. She was free of the hospital at last! If everything went according to plan, she would soon be free of the medical bills as well. And she had a thousand dollars cash in her purse. She glanced at the clock again. Then she felt her wrist. She had no idea what had happened to her watch. Maybe it flew off in the accident. Maybe it got lost during one of the room changes at the hospital. No matter. She now had the money to replace it. And sunglasses! She needed sunglasses. She gathered her bag and tiptoed out of her room.

The wall of windows was curtained for the moment, leaving the big room dimly lit. For the first time, it looked no more special than any hotel room. It needed that expansive view to provide the sense of elegance and luxury. She moved quietly the length of the room. Two other sets of double doors were visible along a corridor on the other side of the suite. Undoubtedly one was to Kevin's room and one was for the chauffeur.

No one stirred.

Her stomach rumbled. A quick search of the well supplied bar revealed a sparkling chrome toaster but no bread or bagels.

That was all the excuse she needed. She scribbled a note at the bar on the bottom of the page where she'd made suggestions for the prenup to let Kevin know she was out. The door to the private elevator was closed. She opened it carefully and pulled it silently shut behind her. Then she pushed the call button for the elevator. The doors opened at once. Suppressing a giggle, she got in and hit the button for the lobby.

She was hungry, but not just for food. When she got to the lobby, things were quiet. It was only six-forty on a Sunday morning. Outside, Monday's rush hour traffic was just a promise. She couldn't stay inside. She had to walk! She moved through the revolving doors and took a deep breath on the sidewalk. The brisk morning air was a delight. She was smack dab in the heart of the city! She didn't have to breakfast in the hotel. She would walk until she saw a place that appealed to her.

Thirty minutes later, she found herself peering through a window at a cute little pastry shop with ice cream parlor chairs and tables, and a clientele dressed for the weekend and exercise, having a coffee before running their miles or unwinding afterward.

With a secret smile, she joined them. She picked out a chocolate chip bagel and ordered a small coffee to go with it. Sitting in the little bakery and watching non-medical personnel going about their day filled her with joy. Once again she was overwhelmed with gratitude at having come out of the hospital a whole person.

And then the memory of the bills and the billing office tried to sour her experience. But she wouldn't let them. She pushed those thoughts away. She was already taking care of her situation. She had made a tough decision to marry a man she knew nothing about so she could put her life in order.

Marry a man she didn't know.

All the hustle and bustle around her dropped away as she realized what those words meant. But she was desperate. And so was he. They were a perfect match, in equally desperate financial straits.

A patron came panting through the door and the small breeze sent her napkin fluttering to the floor. Megan realized she'd been daydreaming. How long had she been sitting here? Darn! Still no watch.

"Excuse me, do you have the time?" She asked the woman behind the counter.

"On the wall," she said.

Megan looked around and saw the clock. It was the same pattern as the wallpaper, so she forgave herself for missing it.

Eight o'clock! She needed to get back.

Thirty minutes later she felt winded as she entered the hotel lobby and pressed the call button for the express elevator. Once inside, she pressed the up button, but nothing happened. She pressed a second time, a third time, but still nothing.

Frowning, she approached the registration desk.

"Excuse me," she said. "I'm staying on the 35th floor but the elevator doesn't seem to be working."

The maroon-coated employee eyed her up and down. "Thirty-fifth floor? That's Mr. Wake's suite."

Megan nodded. "Yes. I'm his fiancée."

"Oh? Just run your room key through the slot, then press UP."

"But I—" Megan stopped herself. She was supposed to be a rich man's fiancée, soon to be bride. She pulled herself up to her full height of five-eleven. "I seem to have left my room key behind. Would you mind?"

"One moment." Maroon Coat was still not convinced, but looked more helpful. He picked up the phone and after a moment, spoke. "Mr. Wake? There's a young woman down here who claims to be your fiancée. She says——. Oh, I see. Yes, sir, I'll send her right up." He put the phone down and almost bowed as he spoke to Megan. "Right this way, ma'am."

Megan tossed her hair, suppressed a smile, and followed him to the elevator. He slid a key card, then handed it to her before the doors closed. After they slid shut, Megan laughed out loud.

When the doors opened again, her laughter died on her lips.

Kevin Wake was furious.

Chapter Eleven

"WHERE HAVE YOU BEEN?!" I was worried sick!"

Megan clutched her purse against her chest. "I'm fine. I went for a walk. I left a note."

"Where?!" He spread his arms and turned at the waist to indicate no note in his general vicinity.

Megan pointed at the bar, irritation sharpening her tone. "Did you look on the bar? Where the paper and pens happen to be?"

Kevin put his hands on his hips. "I hadn't gotten that far yet. Did anybody see you? What am I saying? The whole freaking world saw you!"

Megan turned a hand over. "You didn't say anything about staying invisible. Besides, so what if people saw me? They don't know who I am! They don't know why I'm here. What's the problem?"

Jeffrey Wong stood up from the sofa and a room service tray covered with croissants and coffee cups and two carafes.

"He was worried that one of his father's spies might have seen you."

Kevin shot Jeffrey a warning look, and Jeff put his chauffeur's cap on and saluted.

Megan laughed.

Kevin snorted.

Megan said, "You are really quite attractive when you're angry. But if you do this often, I may think twice about signing that prenup."

Kevin took a deep breath and tried to calm down. "This is too big a deal to take chances that my old man might have people keeping an eye on me, and that includes you now as well."

Megan moved coolly past him and into the big room. As if he had asked about her well being, she said, "I'm doing much better, thank you. The walk in the fresh air did me a lot of good. And I was not approached by anyone."

"Not followed?"

Megan tossed her bag on the sofa and turned her hands out in a question. "I was supposed to be on the lookout for someone following me? You need to communicate more fully, Mr. Wake. Oh, sorry, fiancé Kevin. Anything else I should know? Do you have an old girlfriend who might be pissed off because I'm marrying you? Do you owe money to the Mafia? Are you in the Witness Protection program?"

"Very funny," said Kevin, mollified.

"No, seriously. You are the most paranoid person I ever met. Should I be giving you back your thousand dollars and getting out while the getting is good?"

"No, please. Stay," said Kevin. "You're right. I *am* paranoid. I just lost it when I couldn't find you this morning."

"You were asleep when I left. Do we need to write that into the agreement? Me telling you my every move? If that's part of the job, I'll do what I have to do."

A cell phone rang.

Megan said, "Don't look at me. No phone, remember?"

"Not mine either," said Kevin.

Jeffrey patted his pockets. "Sorry, it's me. Excuse me, Mr. Wake. I have to take this call." He slipped away in the direction of his room.

Kevin said, "We'll get you a cell phone today. It's on my list." He glanced at his watch. "Patrick will be here soon. Then we can get this show on the road."

Megan decided the fireworks were over. She poured herself a cup of coffee. It was lukewarm, but she didn't care. "Are we flying to your summer place in the morning?"

"Jeffrey will be flying. You and I will be driving."

Megan felt her insides twisting at the thought. "There's something I have to tell you," she said. "I hope it's not a deal breaker."

"Go on."

"Ever since my accident, the idea of getting behind the wheel of a car terrifies me. Sweaty palms, butterflies. In fact, more like stampeding ibexes."

Kevin laughed out loud. "Oh, I'm sorry. But, ibexes? Where did that come from?"

"I watched a lot of nature shows in the hospital."

"Well, don't worry. I'll do the driving. Er, you still have a valid license, don't you?"

Megan frowned. "Yes, I do. It's good for another year. But I don't understand why we don't fly. You're rich. Don't you have a private plane?"

Kevin's good cheer faded. "My *father* has a private jet. *We* are driving to Colorado. As soon as we get there, we should get our marriage license."

"Driving to Colorado? The two of us? Without Jeffrey?"

Kevin's features twisted in a question. "You are about to sign a prenup agreement to marry me, but you're worried about us traveling together for a couple of days?"

Megan tossed her hair. "Well, if we're going to be traveling together, maybe we should get married in Reno on the way. Then we can legally register as man and wife, and add more ammunition to this war you're waging with your father." *And I can rest assured that our agreement takes effect without waiting until the end of the month!*

Kevin looked thoughtful. "That might be a good idea. In fact, that's a very good idea."

The elevator pinged on the other side of the door.

"Patrick's a few minutes early. That's good. We have a lot to do today."

Jeffrey emerged from the other room. "Shall I get the limo ready?"

"Not yet," said Kevin. "Patrick's here. We'll need you as a witness for the prenup."

The next hour was a blur of legalese and signatures. Megan got through it only because she could finally see Kevin's promise to pay off her medical bills in black and white, with his signature and initials on every page. The first leg of her mission was accomplished.

When they were done and Patrick had left, Kevin sent Jeffrey to prepare the limo.

Megan spent a few minutes in her room, freshening up. She couldn't get the worry about driving to Colorado out of her mind. It sounded like a very long trip, and she wasn't sure her leg could tolerate it. She would try to talk to Kevin about it again. When she returned to the great room, Kevin was on the phone. Megan entertained herself by nibbling at a croissant.

Kevin hung up. "They're ready for us at the bank. Um, they're going to expect me to walk in with my fiancée. Are you up to faking some affection?"

Megan smiled brightly. "Would you like me to cling? Or just stare at you adoringly from arm's length?"

Kevin chuckled. "Let's play it by ear."

Chapter Twelve

FOR ONCE, KEVIN WAS GRATEFUL for his mother's wealth and connections. The bank president was circumspect and obsequious. He asked no questions, except to request Kevin's identification and the information required to retrieve his safe deposit box.

Alone in the little room with Megan at his side, Kevin opened the long box and set aside a small stack of thousand dollar bills in order to retrieve four bundles of hundreds.

Megan's eyes widened. "I've never seen a thousand dollar bill," she whispered.

"You don't have to whisper."

Megan pulled her shoulders up around her ears. "It just feels so reverential in here."

Kevin grunted. "It's sort of a banker's holy room," he quipped.

"Grover Cleveland? People would remember him better if he were on a common bill. Like Ben Franklin on the hundred. Oh, those are pretty and new."

Kevin nodded.

"Why are the thousands old looking?"

"Because the treasury doesn't issue them anymore. These are still legal tender, but they're not new bills."

"So how much cash is this?" she asked, nodding at the crisp new hundreds.

"Forty thousand. I need pocket money."

His impression of Megan improved with each passing hour. If forty thousand in cash impressed her, she didn't say so. Nor did she ask what he needed it for. She was dignified and attractive. In fact, she was very attractive, and even in her casual capris and sleeveless top, she drew stares from other men. Kevin enjoyed that.

With a couple thousand in cash in his wallet and the rest in his brief case, he enjoyed their next stop on 4th Avenue, where they chose her phone.

"Something simple will do," said Megan.

"No, it won't." He addressed the salesman. "I'd like my fiancée to have the top of the line model, voice assistant, GPS, everything you've got. And can we sync it to mine?" He laid his iPhone on the counter. "Sort of a romantic gesture," he added. "The monthly billing will be added to my account, but I'll pay cash for the phone."

"No problem," said the salesman. "Would you like to browse the accessories?"

An hour later they were back in the limo. Megan was as excited as a little girl facing a tower of birthday presents as she tapped app after app on her iPhone screen.

"It's a camera, too! And a video recorder! Oh, there's a notepad. And look! You can even use it as a phone!"

Kevin laughed. "Don't tell me. You could never afford a smartphone."

"Never. Believe it or not, I spent my first two years at college using the computer labs for typing up my papers because it took me a while to save the money for a laptop."

"Wow. I am impressed." *And a little embarrassed*, he thought to himself, wondering what she would think when she met his eight-year-old brother and saw the collection of techno gadgets he had already acquired.

Megan waved his comment away. "Impressed by poverty? Really? Poor people are not impressed by it, believe me."

"Well, maybe by your thriftiness, then, and your resolve to wait until you saved enough money."

Megan tilted her head to one side. "Okay. You can be impressed by that, because frankly, so was I." She smiled. "I just didn't want to grab one of those credit cards on campus and end up in debt before I graduated."

"Ah, yes. You abhor debt. That's why you're here." His tone was pleasant with a touch of tease.

"Well, I must say, so far this job has great benefits." She beamed with delight at her new phone.

Kevin pulled a soft drink from the mini fridge as Jeffrey maneuvered through traffic. He offered one to Megan and she accepted.

"By the way," said Kevin, "I think it would be wise if we stopped referring to this as your job. You don't want to slip up when you're around my family. And of course, taking my paranoia into account, we don't want any eavesdroppers to hear you refer to me as your employer. Okay?"

Megan nodded agreeably. "Okay. Good idea." She made her excited-little-girl face again. "*Love* has its benefits." She giggled.

Kevin smiled. Ever since the prenup was signed, Megan had begun to relax, and as she relaxed, her expressions became less guarded. He found her happy face extremely attractive, and he found himself wondering what he could do next to ensure that he would see it again soon.

"It's almost three o'clock. Would you like to pick a restaurant?"

"Oh! I know it's totally touristy, but I never got to go before my accident. Could we spend a little time at the Pike Place Market? If we're leaving tomorrow, who knows when I'll get back, and the only thing I've seen in Seattle is the inside of a hospital. I'm sure we can find a snack there."

Kevin grinned. "Why not?" He pressed the switch to talk to Jeffrey. "Megan would like to see the Pike Street Market," he said. "Would you drop us off at 1st and Pike?"

As they emerged from the limo, Kevin instructed Jeffrey to return in two hours. "We'll be ready for a quiet ride by then," he added to Megan. "And the Market closes at five on Sundays."

"Oh, I'm so excited!"

Kevin couldn't help but admire the handsome picture their reflections offered in passing shop windows. His six-foot-four frame usually meant he stood out from a crowd, but with Megan on his arm, the crowd parted for them. Her face was alight with touristy joy, and he found himself seeing the Market through her eyes and experiencing it as if for the first time.

"Use your phone and take some pictures," said Kevin.

"That's a great idea," said Megan. She held the phone up, pressed the camera app, and stared with a frown at the screen. "What do I press to take a picture?"

Kevin angled to stand behind her and gave instructions over her shoulder. "There, that's it. Just press right there."

She did so.

Kevin cleared his throat. "You just took a picture of your feet. It helps if you aim the camera at something not so easy to carry around with you."

"Very funny," said Megan. "At least I can say my feet were at Pike Place Market."

"Try again."

Megan clicked off a series of photos in a circle. Then she said, "Oh, we need someone to take a picture of us together."

Kevin touched another spot on the screen and Megan was looking at her own face. She shrieked with delight.

"Here, you do it! My arms aren't long enough."

Kevin took the phone and held up up in front of them, centered their images and made sure to include the Public Market sign right over their heads.

"That's perfect," said Megan.

The aroma of fish and saltwater from Elliot Bay permeated everything. Before they moved on to the food vendors, Megan bought herself a couple of post cards and a plastic key ring shaped like a salmon.

"I need a tee shirt!" she cried as they rounded a corner into yet another gift shop. "The gaudier, the better."

Kevin picked out a pink girl's tee with Pike Place Market emblazoned across the front. "How's this?"

"Perfect!" She sighed happily. "Okay, we can eat now. I have now officially been there, done that, and—"

Kevin joined her in the chorus, "—bought the tee shirt!"

They laughed together and Megan leaned into him and looked up into his eyes with genuine affection.

The moment was over too soon for Kevin. But he made a mental note of yet another expression of Megan's that he wanted to experience again.

They were pulling into the hotel parking garage when he realized he'd forgotten to check out her hospital story.

Chapter Thirteen

MEGAN RUSHED AHEAD OF KEVIN into the suite and down the hall to her room.

"Be back soon!"

She didn't want to be any more specific than that. Fiancée or not, sometimes a girl just needed privacy.

A few minutes later, she collapsed on her bed and let the day's events do reruns through her mind. The iPhone was a delight. She picked it up and reviewed the photos they had taken. When she got to the one that Kevin had taken of the two of them, her breath caught in her throat.

Megan's first thought was, what a lovely couple. Then in an instant, she realized that she was part of that couple and Kevin was devastatingly handsome! Was it because he was so photogenic? Or was it because he seemed to be having as good a time as she was at the Market? His smile lit up the little screen, dimmed only by her own. They really did look like a couple in love.

Odd that a man of his wealth and standing did not zip around the country on a private plane. She could understand that he didn't want to use his father's jet, but he was a big boy. He could buy his own. Couldn't he?

Megan sat up on the edge of the bed. Maybe she should ask him about that. And there was another matter that needed addressing. She had purchased clothes, but had no luggage to pack them in. She'd better tell him soon, because he expected them to leave in the morning.

She left her room quietly, her footfalls muffled by the thick carpet and headed toward the great room. The sound of Kevin's voice raised in anger gave her pause, and she stopped to listen from the hallway.

"I'm doing the best I can," he grouched. "And you need to stop calling me. You know what the lawyers will make of that. I'm handling it!"

He snapped the phone shut.

Jeffrey said, "She's just trying to help."

"I know, but talking to her makes me crazy. Things were humming along so smoothly. Then she calls, and everything falls apart."

"Oh, really? You were living in a one-room apartment, barely keeping body and soul together. That's what you call humming along? I call it running away from reality. Holing up. Hiding out."

"Big words from a man whose paychecks I sign."

"Very funny. And as for getting *her* out of your life, we both know that's not why you ran. *She* was never your real problem."

Megan turned silently in the hall and tip-toed back to her room. Once inside, she closed the door and leaned against it. Her heart was thumping against her breast bone.

"I knew it," she whispered, "I just knew it! Too good to be true. He's trying to trick me into something. Why would he be living in a one-room apartment if he were really rich?" She began to pace. "But he really is rich! That banker let him in on a Sunday. And he pulled forty thousand dollars of pocket money out of his safe deposit box! Maybe he's just eccentric. A wealthy eccentric would have a hide-away. Oh, mama, what have I gotten into? And I already signed that darn document." She chewed her knuckles. "Well, I'll just have to confront him. Tell him I want out."

She groaned.

"But I want him to pay my medical bills! He signed, too, darn it. If I'm bound by that document, so is he. And if I don't marry him, he won't have to keep his end of the bargain." She took a deep breath and let it out.

Then she thought of something else. "He was talking about another woman! So there must be some crazy ex out there waiting to claw my eyes out."

She paced some more. But no amount of pacing solved her luggage problem. She decided she would have to go out there and ask her questions and get it over with. Once more, with great resolve, she exited her room.

She didn't take a chance on overhearing any more bad news. She cleared her throat loudly as she approached the great room, and called out, "Excuse me!"

Kevin turned from his spot at the wall of windows.

"Oh, hi, Megan. Did you get enough to eat at the Market? I was thinking of ordering a snack from room service."

Afraid she would lose her momentum, Megan blurted out what was on her mind. "I overheard you talking to Jeffrey. I came out to ask if you have suitcases I can use to pack my things in. And I heard you two talking. Was I right? Do you have some crazy ex-girlfriend stalking you and lying in wait for me somewhere?"

Kevin's look of puzzlement graduated to bewilderment. "Ex-girlfriend? No. I don't have a clue what you're—"

She cut him off short. "Jeffrey said you're running away from a woman."

"Oh," said Kevin. "Oh, that. No, no, that was not an ex-girlfriend. I was on the phone talking to my mother. Jeffrey said I was running away from my *mother*."

Megan deflated. "Your mother?"

Kevin nodded. "She's a tad possessive. You need suitcases? There are three for you behind the bar. I'm getting ready to call room service. Last chance for a snack." He gave her a boyish look.

Megan had to smile. She wished he looked like that all the time, like that happy man she'd played tourist with. "Oh, what the heck. Onion rings and chocolate ice cream, please."

Kevin grinned. "Excellent."

Megan looked around. "Jeffrey went to bed already?"

"No. He's running an errand. Did you have fun today?"

Megan relaxed at the thought of their excursion. "I had a ball. When we're all done with things at the ranch, can we come back and play tourist again?"

"Sure," said Kevin. "Even if I can't, you certainly can. Once we get through the end of the month, you can do all the tourism you want."

Megan felt unaccountably disappointed. "Oh, that's right. I thought you might need me to hang around for a while as your wife."

Kevin thought about that for a moment. "You know, you're right. I'm really not sure exactly how close we'll need to stay to each other as things play out. Speaking of which, when my mother called, she gave me a list of questions for you. She needs to know these things as soon as possible. She's working on the wedding arrangements." He handed Megan a list. "I'm going to call room service." He moved to the far end of the room.

Megan sat down and read the list. At the top, Kevin had doodled diamonds and other shapes around his mother's name. Then he'd jotted separate items in block letters. Dress size. Height. Inches from waist to floor. Body measurements. Hair and eye color. Ring size. Shoe size. Favorite flower. Favorite color.

His mother was actually taking Megan's tastes into account! She must be in favor of this whole marriage idea. Megan took a pen from the coffee table and began answering the questions.

"I need a tape measure to do this," she said.

"Check the drawers behind the bar. The hotel has thought of everything else. Why not a tape measure?"

Megan shrugged and checked the drawers. "Hey, you're right! There's a sewing kit in here."

"Told you so."

Megan unrolled the tape measure and placed one end at her waist. Then she dropped the other end to the floor. The kinks in the tape refused to straighten. She smoothed it with her fingers and bent to the floor. As she bent to read it, her measurement from waist to floor got shorter and shorter.

"I think you need to help me with this one."

Kevin dropped ice cubes in a glass, then came to her aid. He dropped to one knee and straightened the tape measure for her.

"There you go. Forty-four inches from waist to floor."

"Thanks. I'll do the rest." She looked down at him. Having him on his knees in front of her stirred feelings deep inside. She cleared her throat and stepped away. "It looks like your mother is going to have a dress made for me."

Kevin stood up. "She said you wouldn't have time or access to the proper stores once you reach the ranch. She'll have a dress sent from New York."

"I hope I get to try it on."

Kevin returned to the bar and filled his glass with water. The ice cubes tinkled as he lifted it and drank.

"Don't worry. Knowing my mother, she'll bring her personal seamstress along to make any adjustments you need."

Megan's eyes widened. "Personal seamstress?"

Kevin didn't seem to think having a personal seamstress was a big deal. "She doesn't like to depend on local availability when she's meeting a deadline."

"Oh, of course not," said Megan, waving that idea aside with a flick of her wrist. She turned away so he couldn't see her eyes roll with disbelief. "I'd better finish this."

She was down to her favorite flower—roses—and favorite colors—berry tones, reds, and pinks—when room service knocked.

Kevin tipped the waiter and rolled the cart of food to the sofa where Megan was sitting.

"I really enjoy the fact that you are not afraid to eat real food," he said.

"Real food is my favorite, and I missed it like crazy in the hospital." She held up the tape measure. "But I should keep this handy. The minute those inches start creeping up, I have to revert to salads and white fish."

Kevin made a bleak face. "That sounds terrible."

"Well, fortunately for both of us, I lost over ten pounds in the hospital. That's why I'm enjoying my food so much. That and the realization that I came way too close to never tasting food again. I'm not sure why, but that thought just makes me hungry!"

"Good." Kevin uncovered the trays on the cart.

Megan inhaled and let her eyes roll blissfully back in her head. "That is so wonderful! Oh, you ordered nachos! May I snag a chip?"

"I'll trade you a cheese laden chip for an onion ring."

"Deal."

"Eat your ice cream first," said Kevin. "It'll melt if you wait."

"Want some?"

Kevin's eyes lit up. "May I?"

"Grab a spoon." Megan held hers upright. "Ready? Go!"

They ate ice cream as fast as they could. When it was all gone, Kevin threw his head back and cried, "Brain freeze! Brain freeze!"

Megan laughed. "Good! You won't see me steal another nacho."

"Oh, no you don't, you little thief." He reached for her wrist and pulled her hand away from the plate.

Megan used her free hand to swipe the nacho. "Amateur!" She turned her face away and stuffed the nacho in her mouth.

"So, it's like that, is it?" Kevin released her wrist and took a handful of onion rings. One by one, he dropped them into his mouth and munched. "Mmmm, so good."

"Oh, yeah? Want some more?" Megan picked up an onion ring and threw it at Kevin's head. It bounced off his cheek. Megan broke into giggles.

Kevin spread his hands and pinned her with a challenging stare. "You know what this means? Your onion ring made contact. The gloves are off, baby. Prepare to defend yourself!" He reached for a nacho and took aim.

Megan looked horrified. "No! No! Not the cheese! These clothes are brand new!"

Kevin stopped short of flinging the nacho. Instead, he popped it into his mouth and chewed.

Megan grabbed a handful of onion rings and hurled them across the table. They caught Kevin in the chest.

He roared like a playful lion and lunged for her.

Megan squealed and ran for the hall at the back of the suite.

Kevin caught her in the hallway and pinned her gently against the wall.

"Oh, you think you're so clever," he said. "Well, let's see how you like it." He pulled an onion ring off his shirt front and taunted her with it, threatening to rub its greasy goodness all over her new outfit.

"No, please," giggled Megan, breathless. "Please don't ruin this outfit! I haven't had new clothes since my sophomore year in college!"

Kevin relented, but only because they were gasping for air. He leaned one palm against the wall and swung the onion ring around his index finger.

Megan squealed with laughter and batted his hand away.

Then their eyes met, and at the same moment, they realized their faces were tantalizingly close.

The laughter faded to smiles, and they stood chest to chest for several seconds, their gazes locked. Drawn together by personal gravity, they leaned toward each other.

He's going to kiss me, thought Megan.

Jeffrey's voice came at the worst possible moment.

"Hey? Where are you guys?"

Kevin pulled away as if Megan were molten lava.

When he did, Megan drooped with disappointment, but she recovered in time to turn the movement into a dive under his arm.

Jeffrey came around the corner. "Am I interrupting something?"

"No, of course not," said Kevin brusquely.

"Don't be silly," added Megan.

"We were just discussing—" Kevin searched for words.

Megan took over. "My wardrobe. And luggage and packing." She added under her breath, "Oh, my."

Kevin pointed a finger at her. "*Wizard of Oz!* I love that movie."

"Me, too," said Megan.

Jeffrey gave them a crooked glance. "Everybody loves that movie."

Megan straightened her sleeveless blouse. "Well, I'd better start packing. I left the answers to your questions on the coffee table, Mr. Wake."

"Kevin," he corrected. "Fiancée, remember?"

Megan nodded. "Sorry. Kevin." She had to force herself to look away before the giggles took over again. "Good night, Jeffrey."

She retreated, stopping behind the bar to snag two suitcases and a makeup bag which would be used as an overnight case since her only makeup items fit tidily into her purse.

Inside her room once again, she realized she hadn't questioned Kevin about Jeffrey's comment regarding his one-room apartment.

"Darn it," she muttered. She flung the empty suitcases on the bed and plopped into the tapestry chair by the writing table. A little card was teepeed next to a phone charger. It read, "Free WiFi for guests."

"My new phone!" She pulled her purse close and dug for her phone. She plugged it in to charge, and then pressed the icon for the internet browser. If Kevin was truly wealthy, there should be information about his family on the internet.

Chapter Fourteen

KEVIN CLEARED HIS THROAT. "So, how did it go?"

Jeffrey grinned. "Thanks for letting me do that. What a thrill! Here." He held up a set of car keys. "You have fifteen days to register it."

"I'm glad you were able to entertain yourself while we did our touristy thing this afternoon."

Jeffrey opened the fridge behind the bar and pulled out a pair of beers.

"Want one? No? Good, because I want two." He popped them open and drained half the first one before continuing the report on his secret mission.

"I went to that Ford dealership you were talking to yesterday afternoon, and found the fellow you told me about. Explained the situation, about you being a wealthy recluse and all that nonsense, and wham, bam, he says pick out a color. Picked a green gem Ford Expedition, by the way. Looks black in the shade, dark green in the sun. Even got to test drive it for you."

"Did you pick out any extras?"

"Oh, yeah! Four-wheel-drive, AC, the usual, but also leather seats, premium sound system, DVD player for the back seat. Park assist, rear sensors, the whole nine yards. Awesome."

Kevin smiled. "Good. You had a good time, then?"

"The best part was tonight. I pulled up in the limo. The fellow from the limo rental was there, just like you arranged for. He took over the limo, and I walked in with the papers you signed before I left. Wham, bam again. Cash really speeds up the new car purchase, you know?"

Kevin chuckled. "My mother has been telling me that for years. She'll be pleased when I tell her she was right." He pocketed the keys. "You have your ticket?"

"Sure do." Jeffrey patted his jacket pocket. "My car is in the parking garage. Sure you don't mind me hanging out in this suite for an extra night?"

"Consider it a bonus," said Kevin. "Just don't break any laws."

Jeffrey grinned from ear to ear.

Kevin returned to the sofa where the room service cart was within reach. He poked through the plates to see if there was anything else he wanted. He lifted one last lid and his eyes glowed with pleasure at the sight of the pastry array.

"Come have coffee and dessert. You have everything you need to get your rental car at the other end?"

"Yep. You sure you want me to keep using your card?"

"Of course. You're on the clock. These are my expenses, not yours."

"Cool." Jeffrey waved off dessert and lifted his second beer in the air. But he settled on the facing sofa, unbuttoned his chauffeur's jacket, and stretched out. "When I came in, it sounded like you and Megan were getting to know each other a little better." He wagged his eyebrows. "Sorry if I interrupted anything."

"Don't be crude. We were laughing, that's all. I *am* allowed to have a laugh or two with my future bride, right?"

"Grumpy, grumpy. Hey, man, how's your sister doing? What is she now, fifteen?"

"Fourteen. She's having a rough time. Trying to find herself. The old man is threatening to send her to a finishing school in Geneva. That's the girl equivalent of being sent to military school. It would kill her free spirit to go there."

"Free spirit, huh? That's what they call mental illness these days?"

"She's not sick, Jeff. She's just in a phase."

Jeffrey's eyes grew big. "Okay, then. Have you told Megan about your mentally healthy family and all their phases?"

"Smart ass. Not yet. That's the reason we need to drive to Colorado. It'll give me time to educate her about the family. The whole idea is for this wedding to look as real as possible. I don't want my dad's lawyers picking up on any gaps in her knowledge and using that as a lever in a courtroom to suggest I'm just doing this for the trust."

"Right," said Jeffrey. "Whatever you have to tell yourself."

"What does that mean?"

"You and I both know you're terrified of flying, dude."

Kevin made a face. "Well, that is an additional motivator, I admit."

Jeffrey laughed. "You'd better be sure she knows what to expect when she gets to the ranch or you're going to have a mess on your hands."

Kevin's voice was dark and sarcastic. "Gee, thanks for reminding me that this whole charade could get even darker."

Chapter Fifteen

MEGAN TYPED KEVIN'S name into the tiny phone screen. "Wake" turned out to be a fairly uncommon name. She found "wake surfing sites," videos of the band "Wake the Dead," and dozens of references to articles dealing with politics "in the wake of" various gun-related crimes. But no Kevin Wake. She rubbed her eyes. What was Kevin's father's first name? She couldn't remember.

But surely if the Wake family was wealthy and owned a big ranch, wouldn't that show up? She found dozens of real estate listings for ranches for sale, but none of them were associated with the surname Wake.

She took a deep breath and wondered if she should resort to her mother's method for calming her fears. Her mother used to say childhood prayers with her. But without her mother's reassuring presence in the room, Megan didn't think it would work. Then she was instantly ashamed. After growing up in the household of the two most devout people she knew, she felt she should have carried more of their faith away with her. Maybe she would try again after she finished packing.

After all, it wasn't as if she were going to back out of her agreement with Kevin now. She had to go through with this marriage, if for no other reason than she had signed the prenup. Her word was her bond. But beyond that, she desperately wanted her medical bills to be paid and be free of that debt without ruining her financial life before she even got started on a career.

"Think of this as your first job," she said rationally. "You will receive a huge bonus when it's done. Focus on that."

Yes, a huge bonus if Kevin was really a wealthy man. And if he wasn't?

Maybe the trust was on his mother's side of the family. It must be. After all, she was the one who wanted information about Megan's dress size and shoe size so she could get the ball rolling with regard to the wedding on the ranch.

What was his mother's maiden name? Didn't Kevin mentioned it to her during her interview? She squeezed her eyes shut and demanded the interview scene to play in her mind. She used to do that during tests at school, replaying scenes of herself studying a certain topic, and with practice she'd gotten quite good at it. And her old skills did not fail her now. There it was. His mother's name was Fineman. And he had doodled "Krystal" at the top of his list.

She opened her eyes and typed the name into the Google search box. The screen filled with links related to Krystal Fineman Wake. She scrolled to the bottom of the screen. There were over ten pages of links related to Kevin's mother. Dozens of articles had been written about her charitable giving. One of the articles praised her for maintaining her involvement in Colorado ranching while maintaining a home in New York City. A rescue organization for horses devoted an entire page to her donation history. She had also funded special education groups, private schools, and programs to benefit underprivileged children. One such program involved horseback riding as therapy for handicapped kids.

Curious, Megan clicked on the link and found photos of different children perched on the backs of large horses. The kids facial expressions ranged from serene to gleeful. A rugged looking man dressed for working on a ranch was shown leading several of the horses. Megan squinted to read the caption, then remembered that she could enlarge the print with a movement of her fingers. She did so.

The caption read "Zachary King, foreman of the Finemans' Rocking Eagle Ranch, assists a young rider."

"That must be it," said Megan. "Okay, his mother's family owns a ranch and they let kids ride their horses. And she gives lots of money to charity. So he should be able to pay my medical bills." Reassured, she turned the phone off and began packing for her trip to Colorado.

It didn't take as long as she thought it would, because everything she owned, she had purchased the day before. She marveled at how little she had actually acquired. But then, a woman can only do so much in a three hour period at the mall. She hoped she had enough to get her through the next five days. Surely there would be a washer and dryer at the ranch. She sighed wearily.

The thought occurred to her that she could ask Kevin for a bigger clothing allowance, but she cringed at the idea. She didn't want this arrangement to turn her into a scheming, money-centered shopping queen. She'd spent her entire life learning how to get by on what was available.

Then she remembered that she had a thousand in cash in her purse. If she needed more clothes, perhaps she could borrow a car and find the nearest thrift store. Her money would go a long way there.

Smiling to herself and feeling much more confident about Kevin's access to funds, she got ready for bed. She knew he was keeping something from her, possibly several somethings, but he had also signed the prenup, and one thing was certain. He needed to get married before his twenty-fifth birthday or he would lose everything.

Well, he hadn't put it exactly like that, but Megan had the distinct impression that he was at least as desperate as she was. One way or another she would get those medical bills off her back. Her parents would be appalled at the size of those bills.

"Mom!" Megan hadn't called her mother yet! She dug through her purse and found the string of numbers for the Guatemalan home where her parents were staying the last time she'd heard from her mother. She squeezed her eyes shut. "What time is it there?" She glanced at the time display on her phone. "Midnight! Oh, no. I can't call now. It's one a.m. there. I'll wake the whole house." She sighed. "I'll call tomorrow, mom. I promise."

She wondered as she fluffed her pillow how long they would stay married. Clearly, they would each be expecting to separate at some point and get on with their own lives. She wanted to find a good man for herself, one that never yelled the way her father did. She wanted a man who was strong but gentle, the way Kevin was in the Market, helping her navigate the crowds. She wanted a man with a sense of humor, someone to laugh with. Just like she'd been laughing with Kevin when he threatened her blouse with his onion ring.

As sleep dragged her into dreamland, she realized with a tickle of surprise that she wanted a man just like Kevin.

Chapter Sixteen

Monday, June 25

KEVIN WOKE UP AT THE first ugly beep of the hotel alarm clock. It was the second worst way to wake up. The first worst was by the ringing of a phone, so he hadn't requested a wake-up call. His backup was his phone, and by the time he swung his legs over the side of the bed, his phone began singing to him. He turned it off on his way to the shower.

He'd arranged for early morning coffee and breakfast before he went to bed. He wanted to enjoy as much of the hotel suite as he could, considering the amount of cash he'd handed over at registration.

But then, by Megan's measuring stick, he was just playing at money worries. He had to admit, she had a point. It never occurred to him that a bankruptcy was a life ruining decision. In the world of business, people did what they had to do and didn't attach any shame or failure to a Chapter 11. At least, people on his father's level gave that impression. And he was embarrassed to admit that he had never given it much thought.

Megan had, though. The burden of her debt was not yet enough to send her to a bankruptcy lawyer. She didn't even want to consider the possibility. He was amazed that she had worked two jobs to get through school. He had to admire her character. And to be honest, he was reassured by the fact that she was so scrupulous about money.

And yet, such a focus on finances could mean that he'd been right from the first. She could still be planning to work some kind of blackmail on him.

As he soaped and rinsed and shampooed, he chided himself for his lingering doubts. Was this another gift from his old man? Would he go through life suspecting everyone of wanting to get their hands on his money?

He snorted. It wasn't his yet. And it wouldn't be his, until he and Megan were married. What if she changed her mind? He would be powerless to help his sister and kid brother if this thing fell through. And what if his old man found a way to scare her off? Or worse?

Kevin picked out his clothes with a road trip in mind. He'd been up late packing his bags. A part of him wanted to run by his one-room apartment before he left town, but that would give his situation away, and he couldn't risk that. No, if he needed anything along the way, he'd just shell out more of his hoarded allowance.

He'd asked his mother the night before about extra funding.

"I may need some financial backup on this, mother."

"You've been hoarding everything I sent you for a long time, Kevin. That's more than enough to attract a bride. Your primary mission is to get her to the ranch. Once you're here, I can slip you whatever you need. But I will not do a bank transfer that your father can chase down. I refuse to give him any more ammunition against you."

"How do you know I've been saving it?"

"The same way your father will know if I send you any extra."

The memory of that conversation only strengthened his determination to prove his father wrong. Was there any part of his life that his old man could not spy on?

He slipped into a pair of his favorite faded jeans and an olive tee, but he hesitated about his shoes. He'd gotten very comfortable wearing running shoes all day, every day, but for once in his life he wasn't trying to fit in as an ordinary guy. He actually needed people to perceive him as the man his mother wanted him to be. With a groan of protest at the necessity, he slipped his feet into a pair of expensive Italian loafers.

He'd forgotten how comfy they were. Okay, so it wasn't too big a sacrifice.

He glanced at the clock. Seven a.m. Still time too check email.

He smiled at the memory of their food fight as he left his suite. He'd captured her right there, next to his bedroom door. She had a very pleasant laugh, and seemed to be genuinely having fun. He warmed at the thought of her lips so close to his. It was probably for the best that Jeffrey interrupted them. He shouldn't get too involved. He couldn't let himself be pulled into a situation where he actually cared about Megan. That would make ending their charade much more difficult. He needed to look at the whole situation like a business deal. Just like his father would.

He heard a soft knock at the door. Room service was right on time. He tipped the waiter and poured himself a cup of coffee. The aroma soothed him. He picked a maple bar off the platter. The cloying sweetness was the perfect mate to the coffee. He opened his laptop and settled on a chair as it warmed up.

When he went away to college, his sister Karla had only been seven years old and his baby brother Keegan was literally a baby. He saw them sporadically over the years, always when his father was away in Europe or when his mother took them to the ranch for summer vacation. He'd even managed to spend a few Christmases with them, again at the ranch, because Douglas Wake had grown fond of spending his holidays abroad. He called them "working holidays" and claimed that trying to do business with the children underfoot was pointless.

Karla worshipped her brother, and for over a year she'd been hinting that he should let her come visit him in Seattle. More recently she even hinted that she might show up unannounced, because things were becoming more and more difficult at home. Whether their father was around or not, he insisted on controlling her life with heavy-handed threats about special schools for unruly girls. Karla was looking for a way out, and Kevin was worried sick that her behavior was escalating along with her desperation. But bringing her to Seattle, even for a brief visit, would only aggravate his father further. In addition, with a one-room apartment and the hours he worked, he wasn't comfortable with that idea. She was fourteen now and needed her privacy. For that matter, so did he. When this was all over, he would do more for her. If he had to give up his freedom to ensure his siblings' future, he should at least allow himself a comfortable home, a place where his troubled sister could find refuge.

Kevin had three different email accounts. He used one for those rare occasions when his father had to communicate with him. The second one was his general email account. And the third was reserved for reaching out to Karla. He checked that account first.

Karla had sent him an attachment. He smiled. Sometimes she would chronicle her life on her phone, then send him an illustrated journal. This email had only one photo attached. He clicked on "download."

The photo popped up on his screen.

The smile froze on Kevin's face. His pleasant anticipation faded to grim concern. The photo was captioned, "Self portrait."

"Oh, Karla," he groaned, "what are you doing to yourself?"

Chapter Seventeen

MEGAN POPPED OUT OF BED before her alarm sounded. She picked out a pair of pale green capris to go with the touristy tee she'd bought the day before. It made her smile, and she needed all the good humor she could get if she wanted to survive her business arrangement.

She showered and dressed quickly, but took her time with her hair. In the hospital, she'd despaired that it might fall out. It just seemed limp and lifeless no matter what she did. But now, it fluffed beneath the blow dryer and looked thicker with every stroke of the brush. If this kept up, she would once again cherish it as her best feature.

She double-checked her baggage, made sure her phone and charging cord were safely tucked away in her purse, and took a moment to apply her lip gloss. Then she gave herself a once-over in the mirror. Shoulders back, nose elevated an inch or so, just enough to allow her to look down on the world. She laughed out loud. Yes, she was ready to play the part of a rich man's wife.

She picked up her purse, and the packet of medical bills crackled inside it. Her smile faded. Somehow, she would find a way to get Kevin to make good on this marriage business right away. A lot could happen in a week. What if he changed his mind? What if he dropped dead from a heart attack or had a freak accident? The knot of worry was back, banging its ugly head against her insides.

Or perhaps she was hungry. She could swear she smelled coffee. She decided to take her things to the great room. There must be a coffee pot behind that bar.

She piled her suitcases one atop the other and clutched her overnight bag and her purse in the other hand. The carpet made her progress down the hall completely soundless. When she reached the entryway, she left her bags and moved into the great room.

Kevin was sitting at the table, staring at the screen of his laptop. She wasn't sure, but he looked upset.

"Good morning," she said.

Kevin slapped the laptop shut and lifted his head. "Oh. Hi."

"Mind if I share that coffee? It smells great."

"Sure. Help yourself."

Megan's brow furrowed. "Is everything okay?"

"Yeah, fine."

Megan poured herself a cup of coffee and examined the pastries on the tray. Maple bars, apple fritters, and croissants. At least a dozen. Maybe her concern about a sudden heart attack wasn't far off the mark. She chose an apple fritter and settled on a chair opposite Kevin.

His thick dark hair was wavy in front. She hadn't noticed that before. His hazel eyes looked green in this light. His square jaw was firmly set, as if he were sinking his teeth into a problem.

Megan let the silence of the room do her work. Before long, Kevin sighed and offered, "There's something you should know before we get to the ranch."

"Go on."

Kevin's gaze shifted right, left, up and down, searching for the words he needed. Whatever she needed to know was not easy for him to say.

Megan asked, "Something about your family?"

Kevin nodded.

Okay, thought Megan. *Twenty questions it is.* "About your father?"

"No, not him." Kevin made a disgusted noise. "He's a lost cause."

"Your mother, then."

He shook his head. "No, she's okay. It's my sister Karla."

"What about her?"

"She's—not well."

"Oh?"

"She's been having a lot of problems. Teen stuff mostly, but during the last year or so, she's teetered on the edge of—" He dropped his chin and studied his lap. Then he shifted his gaze to the wall of drapes. "My mother thinks she's mentally ill."

Megan replied as neutrally as she could. "Okay. Every family has problems."

"Just promise me, when you meet her, you won't run the other way."

Megan pulled a bite of apple fritter free and held it at the ready. "I promise." She popped the bite in her mouth.

"No, really. I'm serious."

Megan chewed and swallowed. "And I promised. I will not run the other way. What time are we leaving?"

Kevin didn't look very reassured, but he checked his watch. "I want to miss the morning rush hour. How about 8:30?"

"Excellent." Megan picked up her coffee and balanced what was left of her fritter on the saucer. "I'll go enjoy my room as long as possible." She retreated to her room, snagging her purse on the way.

Once inside, she settled her coffee and fritter on the table and pulled her phone out of her purse. She wanted to check routes from Seattle to—

"Darn it! I don't even know where we're going in Colorado."

She frowned at the tiny screen. It occurred to her that they were going to be on the road a very long time. Way too long. She would need to take breaks. Her leg was already aching from two days of unaccustomed activity. She dreaded the thought of sitting for long days, then trying to walk afterward. She typed in a question. "How many hours to drive from Seattle to Denver?" She picked Denver because she didn't know exactly where they were going.

The answer was 1,333 miles, and a time of 20 hours and 30 minutes if they drove non-stop and encountered no rush hours and no road construction!

Megan slumped in her chair. She could not spend 20 hours in a car. She was a girl! Girls had to pee! Two ten hour days would still be torture. For Megan to be comfortable, it would have to be a three day trip. And that was a long time to be in a car with a man she hardly knew. What was Kevin thinking? Twenty hours, and probably more, was way too long a trip. This was why airplanes were invented, for Pete's sake. She would have to think of something.

Meanwhile, she had to call her mother.

She retrieved the Guatemalan phone number and dialed. She frowned when the only response was a strange bee-bop, bee-bop, bee-bop sound at the other end. Maybe that was their busy signal? She couldn't remember. Had she ever gotten a busy signal before?

She dialed again. Same response.

She made a face at the phone. "I know, I know, it's not your fault. But what the heck is going on?"

It was eight-twenty. She needed to leave. She tried one more time.

Boop, boop. Boop, boop.

That was better. That's what the tone was the last time she called. A male voice answered. "*Aló?*"

"Hello," said Megan. Then slowly, "*Señora* Mully, *por favor?*"

"Ahhh," said the man. Then he let loose a string of Spanish that was unintelligible to Megan.

"I'm sorry," she said. "I'm calling from the United States for Mrs. Mully. Glenda Mully."

"Ahhh." There was a long pause. Then in very stilted English, "Galinda no live here." He hung up.

"What!?" Megan stared at her phone. "That's impossible!" She dialed the number again.

"*Aló?*" Same voice.

"Hello," she said slowly. "Glenda Mully?"

Now the man's voice became irritated. "No, no Galinda here. They change house! *Adiós pues.*"

"Goodbye," said Megan softly. She ended the call and sat glumly, staring into space. For the first time since her mother left her bedside at the hospital, she felt completely empty.

Chapter Eighteen

KEVIN KNOCKED ON MEGAN'S DOOR.

"Are you ready to go?"

After a few moments, Megan opened the door. She did not look happy.

Kevin frowned. "Something wrong?"

Megan moved efficiently toward the entry way. "Now that you ask, yes, there is something wrong."

Kevin followed her. "What now? Another change to the prenup?"

Megan toss her hair back. "Do you know how long it takes to drive to Colorado?"

Kevin shrugged. "A couple of days."

"Two ten-hour days if we don't stop at any restrooms or stop to eat along the way. Two long, miserable days of staring at the passing countryside, and since restrooms and food are a necessity, it's more like two thirteen hour days in the car. That is crazy!"

"How come you're suddenly a road map expert?"

Megan held up her smart phone. "I looked it up. You want this relationship to look real, correct? Well, no bride-to-be would spend the days before her wedding driving cross country so she could arrive to meet her in-laws looking like something the cat dragged in."

Kevin was taken aback. "I bought a brand new SUV to travel in. It's got that new car smell and it's very roomy."

Megan rolled her eyes. "New car smell? Trust me, after three days of driving, you will never want to smell that aroma again. And three days would be the shortest estimate, because I cannot sit in one position for hours at a time." She looked around for her luggage. "Where are my things?"

Kevin resisted the urge to snap, *You mean, the things I bought you?* Instead he said calmly, "Jeffrey took them downstairs and put them in the car. Look, Megan, I thought a road trip would give us an opportunity to get to know each other."

She glared at him. "Let me give you the crash course. I'm a girl. Girls need restrooms on a regular basis. I also need to exercise my legs every couple of hours because of my injury. Otherwise, I get sore and achy. And that makes me cranky."

Kevin decided to play the sympathy card. "Okay, I'll level with you. I'm terrified of flying, all right? I just can't get on a plane. I know it's crazy, but I've tried, and it's real embarrassing when they have to take the plane back to the gate because I'm freaking out. Get the picture?"

Megan appeared to soften a bit. Kevin thought she would relent.

Instead, Megan said, "I'm sorry you have such a terrible fear. Fine. Here's what we'll do. You take me to the airport and I will fly to Reno and wait for you there. It's only twelve hours. I checked on-line. If you can drive to Denver in two days, you can do twelve hours in your sleep. You drive down, we'll get married, and then we'll discuss the rest of the trip to Colorado."

"But I have this beautiful new car!"

"Yes, and you're dying to play with it. I get that. But I have to look after my health. When you first mentioned that we would be driving, it didn't click for me exactly how far we have to go. With me along, we won't get to your ranch until late Wednesday night at best. I will be exhausted all day Thursday, and your mother has scheduled the wedding for Friday. Not good. And trust me, if we spend three days in a car together, neither of us will feel like walking down the aisle when we get to Colorado."

Kevin worked his jaw. "All right. Fine. But if I take you to the airport, it will add two hours to my driving time."

"You have a chauffeur. Jeffrey can take me in the limo."

Kevin cursed silently. He thought fast. "The limo is being serviced. I didn't expect to need it to day. It's up on a rack right about now. And it's Jeffrey's day off."

"You just said he was loading the bags in the car."

Kevin backtracked. "He's supposed to have the day off once we leave."

"Fine. I'll take a cab. And I still have the thousand you gave me. That should get me to Reno. I will meet you there." She powered past him and slammed her hand against the elevator call button.

Kevin spread his hands. "Hey, hey, hey. If you want to fly, you can fly. If you want to get married in Reno, we can do that, too. I don't have time to find someone else to fill your shoes."

Megan tilted her head and said sarcastically, "That's so romantic." The doors opened and she stepped inside.

Kevin put out an arm and kept the doors from closing. "Megan!"

Megan straightened her back and stared straight ahead. "What?"

Kevin stepped inside the elevator to ride down with her. "I'll take you to the airport if you'll tell me what's really wrong?"

Megan glanced sideways at him. "What do you mean?"

"You know, me behind the wheel, you in the passenger seat, driving to the place where the planes take off?"

Megan bit back a smile. "Not that part, silly."

"Well, something must have happened between your morning coffee and your desire to fly to Reno. What's going on?"

Megan chewed her bottom lip, then brushed her hair behind one ear. She pulled her phone out of her purse and activated the contacts list. "I tried to call my mother in Guatemala," she said. She handed the phone to Kevin, as if he could make the call work. "But a stranger answered the phone and said my mother didn't live there anymore." Her voice broke.

Chapter Nineteen

"I KNEW IT HAD TO BE SOMETHING." Kevin placed a comforting arm around her shoulders and dropped her phone in his pocket. "And it was stupid of me not to realize that a major road trip might not appeal to someone who is still recovering from injuries sustained in a car crash. I'll make sure you get a first class seat to Reno."

Without thinking, Megan leaned into him. "Thank you. Are you sure you can't fly as well? Don't the drugs help?"

"Drugs? I don't take drugs."

"Really? Mother's doctor told her that all those calm people in the airport are on drugs! He said she should use Xanax whenever she flies."

Kevin looked uneasy. "I don't like the idea of losing control of myself."

"But that's not what it does," said Megan. "Mom told me. She said it just turns off the fear. She feels like a normal person who isn't afraid."

"Well . . ."

"Can you call your doctor? Get a prescription?"

Kevin made a face.

Megan pinned him with a teasing look. "You still want to drive your new car, don't you?"

Kevin's chin dropped to his chest. Busted.

"That's okay. Let's meet in Reno and get married there. We'll figure the rest out after that."

"You seem eager to make it legal."

"Aren't you? You're the one who stands to lose a fortune. What if something happens on the way to Colorado? What if, God forbid, you run your new SUV off the road? What if you're in a coma and can't get married in Colorado? What if…?" She stopped when the elevator doors opened on the garage level. Jeffrey was waiting for them.

"You've made your point," said Kevin. "You're right. The sooner we're married, the better. Reno sounds great."

Jeffrey looked confused. "Change of plans?"

Megan said, "Kevin and I are getting married in Reno. I'm going to fly there and wait for him to join me."

"Mr. Wake, may I have a word with you, please?" Jeffrey pulled Kevin aside.

Megan strolled toward the new Ford Expedition where Jeffrey had been arranging luggage. One of the back doors was still open. She could hear Jeffrey whispering furiously at Kevin. Odd. Maybe it was some urgent chauffeur matter. She took a deep breath and let it out slowly. By this time tomorrow, she could be married and no longer alone with her debts. She hoped the Courthouse in Reno opened for business at eight a.m.

She was relieved that Kevin hadn't fought her on the idea of getting married in Reno. And her logic wasn't totally self-serving. After all, as he said, she'd made good points. She herself was living proof that an instant on the highway could turn ugly. No one was guaranteed a smooth ride through life. If he wanted to protect his inheritance, then he should take every precaution, and getting married as soon as possible was a big one.

She folded her arms against the cool breeze that came down the ramp. Why was it that garages were always chilly? Maybe something in the concrete attracted cold breezes.

Now she could hear Kevin whispering back at Jeffrey, just as fervently. What on earth? Were they negotiating the chauffeur's contract?

"Kevin? Is everything okay?"

A bellboy emerged from an elevator, pushing a luggage-laden cart. Behind him came a family with two chatty children. They barely spared her a glance as they followed the bellboy to their car.

Kevin lifted a hand. "Megan? I need to go back upstairs for a few minutes. Did you want to wait here?"

Megan made a face. "I'll wait in the lobby," she said. She moved to join them in the elevator.

As soon as Megan was inside, Kevin pressed the button for the Lobby and then the express button for his suite. Neither Kevin nor Jeffrey said a word as the elevator rose to the Lobby. Megan stepped out, her purse securely over her shoulder.

"I'll be down in just a minute," said Kevin.

Megan nodded. "I'll be over there by the gift shop."

The doors closed. Before they shut all the way, she heard Jeffrey say, "Don't be an idiot." Then they clicked shut.

Megan frowned. That was a very strange thing for an employee to say to his employer.

Chapter Twenty

"I THINK SHE HEARD YOU."

"So? Make something up," said Jeffrey. "You're the one who said she's a blackmailer who can't be trusted. You're crazy if you let her get on a plane with a thousand dollars of your money! She'll be in Reno by one o'clock and you'll be on the road until nine p.m. All she has to do is turn around in the Reno airport and buy another ticket for somewhere else, or even worse, a bus ticket, and she's gone, and you're screwed! You'll never see her again."

"Well, I can't force her to drive with me all the way to Colorado," said Kevin as the elevator rose. "She just got out of the hospital after a major car wreck. No wonder she wants to fly."

"Then go with her."

"You know I can't do that." Kevin paled. "I'm not proud of being a coward, but you remember what happened last time."

"Yeah. It was humiliating. But I've got the answer."

"If I fly, what about the car? I'm not saying I'm going to, but it's brand new! I'm not leaving it in the hotel parking lot."

"Look, you take this." Jeffrey pulled his airline ticket out of his pocket and handed it to Kevin. "Cash it in when you get to the airport."

"They'll need your I.D. for that."

"I'll be there. I'm driving you."

The elevator doors opened. Jeffrey got out and headed toward the back of the suite. Kevin stepped into the great room and looked around again, trying to soak in every penny's worth of atmosphere.

Jeffrey reappeared and handed Kevin a prescription bottle. "Take one of these now. Just do it. When you get to the loading gate, take a second one. Then get on that plane and don't let Megan out of your sight! I will drive your new car to Colorado."

"Really?"

"No problem."

"You sure these will work?" He read the label. Xanax. "Hey! This is what Megan suggested I use."

"I've been trying to get you to try these since our freshman year. Now's the time. They work. Trust me. How do you think I manage to look like such a fearless flier? If I'm driving the new car to Colorado, I won't need them."

Kevin nodded. "Okay. If you're lying to me, I will never let you forget it."

"I'm not lying. Now let's go. I'll drive you guys to the airport and cash in my ticket for you."

Kevin felt like a man about to face a firing squad. "All right," he said tightly. "Statistics say I should survive the flight."

"And I can invent some statistics that say, if you let go of Megan, you will lose everything. You don't have time to find another candidate. It took three weeks to find *her.*"

"Okay." But Kevin did not feel okay at all.

Jeffrey shook his head and made a rude noise. He opened the pill bottle and shook out a Xanax. "Now, Kev. You have to give it time to work before we reach the airport."

Kevin took the pill and swallowed it dry.

"You ready?" asked Jeffrey.

"Go on down," said Kevin. "There's something I have to do before this pill takes effect."

Jeffrey grinned at him. "You loser. Afraid of flying, afraid of a little pill. Why do I stay friends with you?" He chucked Kevin in the shoulder, then headed down in the elevator.

Kevin pulled out his cell phone and retrieved Megan's from his pocket. He went to the bar and tapped on her contacts list.

There were only two numbers on it, his cell phone number and one for Glenda Mully. That made him sad. No numbers for college friends.

Nothing. Just his number, punched in by him at the phone store, and Megan's mother.

He activated his own phone and tapped in a text message, carefully adding Glenda Mully's number at the end. His finger hovered for a few seconds over the send button. "I hope this isn't a mistake," he muttered as he pressed *Send.* Then he put his phone away, tucked Megan's back in his pocket, and took the elevator downstairs.

The doors opened at the Lobby level. Jeffrey was waiting for him.

"I told you so," said Jeffrey. "She's gone."

Chapter Twenty-One

"SHE'S NOT GONE," SAID KEVIN. "She said she'd be in the gift shop."

"I already looked. I asked the clerk. She said no tall blond woman has been in this morning."

Kevin frowned. "I can't believe it. I *won't* believe it. She's around somewhere. We'll find her."

"Try her cell," said Jeffrey, "if she'll even answer it."

Kevin's brows rose and he pulled Megan's phone out of his pocket. "It won't do much good."

"Oh, great."

Kevin snapped his fingers. "She might think she lost it. She might be looking for it. She would retrace her steps."

"Down to the garage."

"I'll go. You wait here in case she comes up while I'm taking the elevator down." He popped back inside and pressed the button.

When the elevator doors opened, he spotted Megan at once. She was bending low, trying to look under the car.

"Megan!"

Kevin's voice caught her attention. Slowly, she began to rise.

Kevin sped up and offered his hand. Megan took it and let Kevin help her stand upright again.

"Sorry," she said. "Getting up and down is still hard for me. They told me in the hospital it's all in my mind. They said the bone has healed, everything is fine. But it's still hard for me to trust it, going up and down."

"Not a problem." He pulled her cell phone out of his pocket. "Looking for this?"

"Oh, thank goodness!" Megan took the phone and pressed it to her bosom. "I was so afraid I'd lost it! I looked everywhere!"

"You didn't lose it," said Kevin. "When we were in the elevator, you gave it to me when you told me about your mother, and without thinking, I slipped it in my pocket."

Megan tucked it back in her purse. "Did you and Jeffrey work everything out?"

"Er, what do you mean?"

Megan eyed him skeptically. "I heard him call you an idiot. Is he still employed?"

Kevin chuckled. "Yeah, he's still the chauffeur. In fact, let me call him. He's in the Lobby. He thought you took off while we were upstairs."

"What?!"

"You know. A thousand dollars in your pocket, fast money, all that nonsense. He thought you might have cut your losses and left with the cash."

"Not very smart, is he?" Megan tugged at the hem of her top.

"What do you mean?"

"A thousand dollars won't even make a dent in my medical bills."

"Oh, that. Right." He dialed Jeffrey. "I found her. She was looking for her phone by the car. Come on down. We're ready to go." He hung up.

"We?" asked Megan. "I thought you were going to drop me off at the airport on your way out of town."

"Nope. I'm taking your advice. Turns out Jeffrey uses Xanax for flying. I'm going to use his pills so I can fly to Reno with you." He was surprised at how easy that was to say.

"That's great! I'm so glad." Megan's face lit up. "We could be married by this afternoon!"

"Long before I drop dead or fall into a coma."

Megan shot him a look. "Now you're making fun of me."

"No, I'm not," said Kevin innocently. A moment later, he grabbed his chest, and gasped, "Jeffrey better hurry."

"You rat!" Megan swung her bag at him. It caught him in the ribs.

Kevin laughed.

The elevator doors opened and Jeffrey appeared.

"We're ready to go," said Kevin.

"Very well," said Jeffrey, sounding once again like a respectful employee. He held the back door open for Megan. "Miss?"

Megan let Kevin give her a hand up into the back of the SUV. Then he went around the other side and got in beside her.

Jeffrey paused by Kevin's door. Megan was fastening her seatbelt. Jeffrey tucked the pill bottle into Kevin's hand. Kevin shoved it into his jeans pocket. They were off.

Chapter Twenty-Two

MEGAN COULDN'T HELP BUT feel excited when she and Kevin pre-boarded with the other first class passengers. She clutched his arm as a tactic to keep from giggling like a little girl. When they settled into their seats, a very friendly flight attendant offered them drinks. Megan asked for a diet soda and Kevin requested Perrier.

Megan noticed he was clutching the arm of the seat and glancing back nervously at the passengers now boarding for tourist class. She leaned close and whispered, "Take another pill."

"Hmmm? Oh, that's right. I was supposed to take one while we waited for boarding."

"You didn't have time! They sure got us on this flight in a hurry." Megan accepted her soda and sipped at it. "I love this! We get to sit and relax and have a cold drink while the peons are boarding." She spoke with an exaggeratedly snooty voice.

Kevin had to laugh. He swallowed his second Xanax. "I hope these don't make me loopy."

"Did the first one?"

"No." He looked surprised. "No, it didn't."

"But you boarded the plane without panicking."

Kevin nodded. "Amazing. I just hate the idea, though, that I have to take drugs to fly."

"Do you take Tylenol for pain?"

"Yes, but—"

"It's a drug," said Megan teasingly. Then more gently, "You must have some personal experience with the abuse of certain drugs."

Kevin rolled his eyes. "You might say that." He glanced sideways at her. "Hope that doesn't send you running the other way."

"No family is perfect. I assume you'll fill me in as we get closer to the old homestead?"

Kevin made a face, but changed the subject. "Say, you still have your driver's license, right?"

Megan patted her purse. "It's about the only thing I do still have."

"Great. You'll need that in Reno when we get our wedding license. Do you want to be married at the courthouse or in a wedding chapel?"

Megan pondered the question. "I've seen those chapels in the movies, and I wasn't really impressed. Since your mother is preparing an actual wedding for us, let's get married at the courthouse and save the party for your family." She lowered her voice. "That should be a bit less expensive as well."

Kevin agreed.

Megan tucked her purse behind her legs and squirmed in the roomy comfort of the first class seat. She pressed her hands together with delight and leaned toward Kevin. "This is so much fun! You can afford to fly first class, but you were afraid to fly? Gosh, I could understand your fear if you had to fly tourist, but up here?" Her eyes were bright with excitement.

Kevin smiled and took a breath. The Perrier was refreshing. The seat was very comfortable. And the flight attendants were already supplying them with salted nuts.

"Oh, thank you," said Megan effusively.

Kevin patted her knee and said, "My dear, you must learn how to talk to the help. A simple thank you is enough. After all, you are paying for the privilege."

Megan paused, then caught the twinkle in his eye. She punched his arm. "You big pretender! You don't sound nearly hoity-toity enough to be a real snob."

Kevin turned a hand over. "I left home at eighteen, so I'm rusty. Wait until you meet my mother."

Megan said softly, "Oh, goody." Then she whispered, "Do you think it would be tacky to open our nuts while people are still boarding?"

Kevin chuckled. "I think you're allowed. Besides, that's why they board behind us. So they can't see how the upper crust is treated."

Megan tore open the bag of almonds and munched contentedly. When her soda ran out, a flight attendant offered her another.

"Yes, please." She glanced down at Kevin's hands. His fingers were relaxed now, and he was swishing the ice in his Perrier. "Do you drink anything stronger?"

"Hmm? Occasionally. But not very often. That family thing again."

"Got it. Did you put your laptop in the overhead?"

"Yes. Why? Do you need to do more research?" His tone was mildly sarcastic.

Megan shrugged it off. "When I interrupted you for coffee this morning, it looked like something on your computer had upset you."

Kevin looked thoughtful. "My sister. She's having a lot of emotional problems. She sent me a disturbing photo of herself."

"Is she at the ranch?"

"Yes." Kevin seemed to notice the music headphones for the first time and put them on.

When he said no more, Megan dropped the subject. She would meet the troubled sister soon enough. Besides, the doors were closing, and the flight attendants were giving their safety speech. She glanced down at Kevin's hands. They were now tapping in time to music. She allowed herself a tiny smile. No panic attack.

As the plane took off, she noticed that Kevin's eyes were closed and his fingers were still tapping. When the flight attendants announced that people could use their electronic devices again, Kevin got up calmly and retrieved his laptop.

Megan selected a magazine from the basket offered by the flight attendant and thumbed idly through it. Out of the corner of her eye, she kept track of Kevin. When he slammed his laptop shut, she looked up.

"What is it?"

Kevin looked grim. "I have my email program set to save mail to a local file on my computer so I can access it anywhere." He opened the laptop again. "You might as well see this one before we get to Reno." He turned the email so she could read it.

"I know what you're doing. Bring that trollop to Colorado and I won't guarantee her safety."

Chapter Twenty-Three

MEGAN FLASHED WITH ANGER. "What a rude thing to say! Who is this jerk?"

Kevin looked apologetic. "My father."

"Oh, terrific."

"I don't get it! This sounds like he plans to be at the ranch. How can he know what I'm doing? My mother didn't tell him. They barely talk at all."

Megan turned a hand over. "They have children together. Trust me, they talk. Maybe he picked up on a slip of the tongue. Or maybe one of your siblings told him."

Kevin didn't look convinced. "He and my sister are mortal enemies. She clams up whenever he's around. And my kid brother, well, dad keeps telling mother that Keegan needs special education classes. A lot he knows! The kid's a genius!"

"Then maybe he has spies." Megan said it casually, but the effect on Kevin was startling.

He half turned in his seat and tapped a finger on the tray. "I've been saying that for years, and no one believes me! He always sticks his nose in. He always seems to know what I've decided. It drives me crazy."

"Well, who besides your mother knows what we're doing? Do you trust your chauffeur?"

97

"Yes. I've known him for years." But there was a hint of doubt behind the words.

"Then who else?"

Kevin shook his head. "I can't think. It must be the Xanax."

Megan nodded toward the laptop screen. "Is that your father's way of threatening me? Do you think he'll follow through?"

Kevin turned to her. "I won't let anything happen to you. I'm certain he's done things in the name of business that cross the line, but he's mostly bluster. And you'll be in friendly territory. The ranch belongs to my mother's family, and he's never felt comfortable there. He doesn't like the western way of life. Hates animals. Won't let Keegan have a dog at the New York apartment."

"Does he even have a soul?" asked Megan, shocked at the idea of preventing a child from having a pet.

Kevin was taken aback. "You think that's really weird?"

Megan's jaw dropped. "The man hates animals! That is just wrong."

"Well, I'll try to run interference for you if it comes to that. I didn't expect him to be at the wedding, though."

"If he has spies and knows we're planning to get married, and he's against it, I would fully expect him to show up. And as for running interference? You don't come through an accident like mine and six months of fighting for life in the hospital without finding your backbone. Besides, I have a lot of experience with blustery, loud, and pushy fathers. I have one of those myself." She raised a hand for the flight attendant and requested another soft drink.

Kevin sat brooding, staring at his laptop.

"Why don't you put that away and tell me more about your family? You were ready to spend twenty hours in a car filling me in, so you'd better talk fast. It's only two more hours to Reno."

Kevin closed the laptop. "Okay. You already know that Karla is going through a phase."

Megan held up a hand. "Start with your childhood. Where were you born? Who was your favorite teacher? That kind of stuff."

Kevin leaned back in his seat and started talking.

Megan smiled and nodded at appropriate moments. Kevin barely even noticed when the plane landed.

As they strolled through the terminal toward the luggage carousels, Megan nudged him with a friendly elbow. "I think your fear of flying is solved."

Kevin nodded and gave her a half smile. "Yeah, I think you're right. Amazing."

"Maybe we should book our flights to Colorado before we leave the terminal," suggested Megan.

"I already did that in the terminal in Seattle. I rented a car, too, while you were in the ladies' room."

"You're the man," said Megan, slipping her arm around his.

She caught a glimpse of their reflection in the shop windows that lined the terminal and walked a little taller. There was no better looking couple in the whole place. It occurred to her that Kevin had quite a bit of muscle. His olive tee revealed the kind of physique most men had to work at.

"You must be missing your gym workouts," she said.

Kevin shot her a puzzled glance? "Gym? Who has time for the gym?"

It was Megan's turn to look puzzled. "You look like you live there."

Kevin touched his chest in an unconscious gesture. "My summer job," he said enigmatically.

Megan waited, but he said no more.

At last she gave his arm a little pinch. "Which is?"

Kevin looked like a kid caught with his hand in the cookie jar. "Er, I enjoy the outdoors, so in the summer I work as a logger."

"This whole marriage thing must be getting in the way."

"It is interfering with my exercise program," he said. "The luggage carousel is still empty. Let's go to the rental car desk first."

Megan rubbed her leg.

"Did you know you do that every time I mention a car?"

Megan's cheeks burned. "Sorry."

"Don't worry," said Kevin, slipping his arm around her waist. "I've rented a tank."

Chapter Twenty-Four

WITH LUGGAGE IN TOW, Kevin led the way to the rental car lot.

"Wow," said Megan. "I thought you were kidding!"

Kevin grinned at her. "Full size SUV, comes with a step to help you get in and out. Let me load the luggage."

He went around the back and tossed their bags into the rear. Then he opened the passenger door for Megan.

"Thank you, kind sir." She levered herself into the seat.

"I live to serve." Kevin bowed with a flourish.

As they pulled out of the airport, Kevin said, "Let's go take care of business first."

"Fine by me."

An hour later, they were licensed and wed. There was one awkward moment, as they both realized they had no wedding bands to exchange. Kevin explained to the justice of the peace that they were saving the ring exchange for the family celebration.

As they returned to their rental, Megan was very quiet.

"Everything okay?" asked Kevin, opening the door for her again.

"I was just wondering what kind of person you must think I am. How many girls would agree to marry someone just to eliminate a debt?"

"Probably more than you think," said Kevin. "But we're a perfect match. How many guys would agree to marry in order to control the family trust?"

"Thousands," said Megan with a straight face. "Maybe millions."

Kevin laughed. "Yeah, you're probably right. Here, let me help you up."

He got behind the wheel. "Now that we're legal, I want to celebrate. Have you ever been to Reno before?"

"No. I grew up mostly in Cloverdale, California, and my parents would never choose 'sin city' for a vacation." She put finger quotes around it. "That's what my dad calls Reno and Las Vegas."

"What does he call the Indian reservations with casinos?"

Megan shrugged. "No idea."

"Have you ever been to Tahoe?"

"Never."

"Then that's where we'll have dinner."

Kevin concentrated on driving and was quietly pleased that Megan did not chatter all the way up Mount Rose Highway. He noticed that she kept one hand in her purse, fingering the marriage document. Once again, he felt a flickering doubt about Megan. But even if he was right, he could relax. They were married, and he'd managed to find a wife days before his birthday. From what he'd seen of Megan so far, he was certain she would be acceptable to his mother. What his father thought did not matter. Nothing he did would ever please his father, so why try?

Half the battle was won. He would take her home to the ranch for the wedding his mother was organizing. Friday, the wedding. Saturday, his birthday. Monday, meet with the lawyers and take over the Trust. Almost there.

Hang on, Karla. Just a few more days and your future will be secure. Then I can get back to my own life.

He tightened his grip on the steering wheel. *And find out who the spy is.*

As the scenery changed from high desert to forest, Megan began to perk up. By the time they reached Incline Village and Crystal Bay, she was leaning forward, eager to soak in the sights.

"This is beautiful! Everything is nestled among the trees."

Kevin smiled. "I thought you'd like it. Now for the big question. I had to wait until we were legally bound, because your answer could make or break this whole relationship."

Megan grew serious.

Kevin turned away so she couldn't see him fighting a smile. When he could talk, he said, "Do you want dinner in a fancy restaurant? Or a picnic on the beach?"

Megan laughed. "Picnic! Picnic!"

Kevin grinned. "Good choice." He pulled into a steep driveway. It led to an elevated parking lot with a large grocery store and several little shops backed up to the forest.

"I didn't even see this from the road," said Megan. "It all feels hidden away. I half expect to see fairies dancing in the woods."

"No comment," said Kevin. "Let's go get some food. They've got a deli, too."

Kevin pushed the grocery cart and let Megan make the food choices. He found himself watching her with pride. As other men noticed her, he wished he'd thought of a ring sooner, but then, his original plan had not included a quick marriage in Reno.

Megan did a quick examination of the cart. "Chicken, Dr. Pepper, potato salad, enchiladas—" She paused to give Kevin a dubious eye. "— a veggie tray, napkins, paper plates, plastic cutlery, and plastic cups. All done!"

"Not quite." Kevin rolled the cart to the liquor aisle and picked out a bottle of champagne. Then he moved to the in-store bakery and picked out two chocolate eclairs. "*Now* we're done."

By the time they got to the beach, long fingers of shade were stretching along the sand. A cool breeze came off the water. Families and young couples were playing next to the lake. Catamarans danced along the chop.

Kevin found a shady spot and they settled on the sand.

Megan said, "Everyone is dressed for swimming but no one's in the water."

"Go get your feet wet and you'll find out why."

She eyed him suspiciously. "Are there crabs in the water or something?"

Kevin laughed. "No, not at all." He took off his shoes and socks and rolled up his pant legs. "Come on, I'll go with you."

It was obvious she didn't trust him on this, but she got barefoot as well.

Kevin took her hand and led her to the shore, past squealing toddlers and lolling teens. A group of friends was launching a canoe.

Kevin let go of her hand and strode into the clear water, bracing for the impact. He turned a smiling face to her and said, "See? No sharks. No crabs. Come on in."

The boys around the canoe paused to watch.

Megan moved forward cautiously.

Kevin extended a hand. "Here, I'll make sure you don't slip."

Megan took his hand.

Kevin tightened his grip and tugged her forward. Her feet hit the ice cold water and she squealed with surprise.

Kevin laughed out loud. "Mountain run-off, from the snow pack to the lake."

"My feet are freezing!" Megan tried to pull her hand free, but Kevin was having too much fun.

In self defense, she reached down and splashed water at him. As the icy wave hit his tee shirt, he roared and let go of her hand. Megan lost her balance and fell back on her bottom.

The shock of the cold water made her squeal again.

Kevin took pity on her and lifted her by one arm. "Water's fifty degrees."

Megan stood shivering, her capris soaked from the waist down. "Th-th-thanks. I would have g-g-guessed thirty-five!"

A quick return to the SUV for dry clothes was in order. Megan slipped into the ladies' room and came out in a pair of khaki bermudas. She lay her wet capris over a sun-soaked stone to dry as they ate their picnic.

"Sorry about the bath," said Kevin. "I just couldn't resist."

Megan gave him a lopsided smile. "I'm sure I'm not the first girl to have that trick played on her."

Kevin was pleased that she wasn't angry. "Food tastes so much better outdoors."

"I agree," said Megan.

Kevin poured champagne. "I thought we should make a toast to us."

"Great idea." Megan touched her plastic cup to Kevin's. "Here's hoping we both get what we need."

"And want," added Kevin.

They drank.

"Another," said Kevin. "Here's to picnics on the beach."

"I'll drink to that."

They drank.

"One more," said Kevin, smacking his lips and pouring champagne. "Here's to driving the old man crazy by ripping my mother's family money out of his hands."

Megan giggled.

They drank.

"I have to stop," said Kevin. "Or we'll be spending the night on this beach."

"The sun is going down."

"It can't be! We just got here!"

"We landed at two, were married by three, got to Tahoe at four, bought food, found the beach, got wet and cold, lingered over our picnic and you're surprised it's almost eight o'clock?"

Kevin gathered the remnants of their feast and stuffed it into bags. "We'd better get down to Reno and find a room for the night."

"You didn't do that already?" Megan hiccupped.

"No, sorry. But it's Reno. The place is full of hotels. We'll find something."

Megan stretched out on the sand. "We can't stay here and sleep under the stars?"

"Believe me, it will get very cool as soon as the sun sets." He eyed her carefully. "You never drink alcohol, do you?"

"No. How can you tell?" Megan held one finger aloft and began tracing the outlines of puffy white clouds.

Kevin rolled his eyes, but couldn't keep from smiling. "Okay. Here we go. Up and at'em."

"My capris!"

"I'll get them. Can you stand up?"

Megan looked miffed. "I'm fine. It was just a little champagne."

"That's all it takes when you aren't used to it." He reached for the capris.

Megan pointed at a large outcropping of rock that jutted into the water. "Why is that man looking at us through binoculars?"

Kevin whirled around.

The man with binoculars dropped out of sight.

"Did you see him?" asked Megan, with just the hint of a slur.

"Yes," said Kevin coldly. "I did."

Chapter Twenty-Five

SAFELY BACK IN THE RENTAL CAR, Megan felt her buzz fading fast. She glanced over at Kevin. He looked completely sober and super focused.

"You win," she said.

"Excuse me?" He kept his eyes on traffic.

"You win the father competition. Your dad sent that spy, didn't he?

"I think so, yes. He has employees all over the country." He snapped his fingers as a sudden realization hit him. "He must have traced activity on my credit card! Mother said she was worried about his ability to track her financial activity, too."

Megan sighed. "My dad would never do that." Then she shrugged and added lightly, "Probably because he'd consider it too much trouble. But you still win."

Kevin snorted. "That's a win? Great. Lucky me."

"How did this father/son rift start, anyway?"

"He was trying to run my life all the way through high school. Telling me who I could be friends with. Forcing me into private schools. I wanted to see the real world, not the sheltered universe for the children of the mega rich. So I decided to go away to college. Far away. University of Washington."

Megan waved her fingers in the air. "Ooooo, big rebel. Went to an out-of-state university. Skipped Harvard and Yale."

Kevin snapped, "I thought you wanted to hear this story?"

"Sorry. For people in my bracket, a rebel joins a motorcycle gang or becomes a Buddhist monk in Nepal. Going to a school your father doesn't approve of hardly counts."

"It counted in my father's circles. I was turning my back on all the contacts I should be meeting and elbow-rubbing I should be doing at Harvard."

"I get it. Different standard for different classes." She frowned. "Hey, Kevin, do you think your father's spy saw us get married in Reno?"

"No." His reply was immediate.

"That was fast. How can you be so sure?"

"Because we're still in one piece and we actually came out of the building man and wife."

"Yikes. How did his man know we were in Tahoe?"

"Who knows? He probably bribed someone. But we didn't tell anyone we were going to the Lake. That was spur of the moment. And I haven't used my phone." He slapped the steering wheel. "I bet there's a GPS locator on this rental car. If you're not afraid to bend the rules, there are ways to track people."

"No offense, but I don't think I like your father very much."

"It's a big club. Lots of room for new members."

Megan laughed. "That's funny. At least you have a sense of humor about it. Are you club president?"

"Nope. That would be my mother."

Megan didn't know what to say about that, so they rode on silence.

Kevin found them a room at the Sparks Nugget.

Once they reached the room, Megan began to wonder what Kevin would expect of her on their so-called wedding night. She could feel the butterflies starting deep inside, but didn't know if they were caused by nervousness or excitement. After all, he was very handsome. Much more handsome than any of the boys she'd met in college. She didn't run with the popular crowd. She always wound up in the library at a table filled with engineering majors or chemistry study groups. Kevin was only a year older than she was, but he seemed so much more mature than her college acquaintances. It had to be the lumberjack muscles that made the difference. The thought of pressing herself against his bare chest sent the butterflies into a frenzy.

But Kevin did not seem ready to call it a night.

"If you've never been to Reno or Vegas or an Indian casino, you're probably not a gambler, right?"

"Bingo," said Megan. A moment later, "I mean, you're correct. And I don't play Bingo either."

Kevin grinned. He waved her close. "Tonight, you get it all out of your system."

"I don't have it *in* my system."

"Think of it as a kiddie arcade."

Megan's face lit up. "Do they have one of those?"

After an hour at the kiddie arcade, Kevin was impressed by Megan's prowess with the shooting games.

"Where did you learn to do that?"

"One of the jobs I did to work my way through college was at an arcade. I used to be good at the dancing games, too," she said. "But I don't think I'm ready for those yet." Her hand once again dropped to her thigh.

"Ready for the grownup games?"

Megan tensed. The butterflies made another appearance. She could imagine them waiting in the wings with her heart as the stage. But way too many of them were downstairs in her stomach wreaking havoc.

Kevin said, "I mean the slot machines."

"Oh, those! Sure, why not." Megan smiled nervously, and scooted ahead of Kevin so he couldn't see the expression of relief on her face.

The slot machines were entertaining. Megan enjoyed the musical ones the most. Still, she couldn't help but flinch every time Kevin slipped another twenty into the slot. At last she couldn't stand it anymore.

"Let's not waste our money here," she said. "We could have bought wedding bands with what we've stuffed into these machines."

"Good point. Besides, it's getting late and we've got an early flight."

Back in the room, Megan brushed her teeth, put on her pink pajamas, picked one of the beds and crawled under the covers. Kevin disappeared into the bathroom.

Megan leaned back on the pillows and reminded herself that she had walked into this situation with her eyes open and her goal clearly in mind. Part of her had felt nothing but relief since she and Kevin signed the papers at the Courthouse. But another part of her had become increasingly nervous about their first night together.

And there was still the question of where her mother had moved to. And her father as well, of course. Then she felt guilty for not being equally concerned about both of them. She rolled her eyes at herself.

Lying here in bed, waiting for her husband, she had other things to think about besides her parents!

Maybe she should just close her eyes and rest for a moment. It had been an eventful day.

Chapter Twenty-Six

KEVIN SHOWERED TO GET the casino smell off. He dried off and slipped into his pajama bottoms. He wondered if Megan was expecting something romantic this evening. After all, they were married.

"You win," she said.

But Kevin couldn't shake the feeling that having his way with her would be no better than harassing an employee. After all, Megan considered this whole arrangement a job. And how could he make advances on her when she was worried sick about her mother? He could tell she was worried, because she didn't talk his ear off all day. There were far too many long silences during their drive to Tahoe and back.

As he brushed his teeth, he couldn't believe he was concerned about *not* being talked to death. The brief hours they had spent together at the Pike Place Market had shown him a side of Megan that he found genuinely attractive. He wanted his fun-loving tourist back. She had been nervous ever since they got to the hotel.

Or maybe it was because of the man with the binoculars. Maybe she was already regretting what she'd gotten into. He hoped fervently that his father wasn't up to anything violent. Would he go that far?

Yes.

The word came unbidden to his mind. He had suspected for quite some time that his father was more than capable of getting rid of competition or stomping on it so violently that at least one man had committed suicide.

He rifled through his clothes for his cell phone. He opened the bathroom door for a moment, heard the TV droning, and softly closed the door. He could talk safely inside the bath. With the TV on, Megan wouldn't hear anything. He dialed the number of the ranch foreman.

"Zach? Any news?"

"All good. Found the information and made the arrangements. Any other chores for me?"

"No, thanks. That was the one I was worried about."

"I can't wait to meet your fiancée. Am I going to like her?"

Kevin thought for a moment. "Actually, I think you will. Is Karla around?"

"At this hour?"

Kevin realized it was almost one a.m. "Sorry, Zach. My timing stinks."

"No matter. I was still awake. But the main house is dark."

"It will have to wait, then. We fly into Denver at noon, so we should get to the ranch by two."

Zach was silent for a moment. Then, "You? Flying?"

Kevin perched on the edge of the sink. "Yes, me, flying. I finally tried the medicated route, and it helps a lot."

"Want me to pick you up at the airport?"

"Not necessary. I know you must be super busy with mother and the kids there."

Zach grunted into the phone. "You might say that. By the way, I got to warn you. Your sister Karla is plenty upset about this wedding. She said you were her only friend and now you'll shut her out because you'll have a wife."

"She's talking?"

"Only to me."

"As usual," said Kevin. "The poor kid. Try to reassure her, okay? I'm doing this for her."

"Anything else I can help you with?"

"Not at the moment. Any sign of the old man?"

"No, but there's a lot of tension in the main house. And I had to drive into town and refill your mother's prescription."

Kevin made a face. "Not a good sign. How's Keegan?"

"Growing like a weed. Krystal sent him outside to play today, and he sat on a hay bale in the shade with his electronic game. Never looked up. He's angry because he's missing computer camp in the city."

"Terrific. What a lovely mess to drag Megan into."

"Her name is Megan, eh?"

Kevin smiled.

"Well, it's late," said Zach. "I better get to bed. See you tomorrow."

"Good night." Kevin hung up. He would find a way to reassure Karla. He just wasn't sure how yet.

He emerged from the bath and turned off the light. The TV continued to drone on. He stopped for a moment by Megan's bed. She looked like an angel, with her golden hair spread out over the pillow. Their hours at Tahoe had put some pink in her cheeks. Her eyes were closed. She was sound asleep.

Chapter Twenty-Seven

Tuesday, June 26

THE FLIGHT FROM RENO to Denver was uneventful. Megan wondered if she could find other excuses to fly first class as Kevin's wife. The price of their tickets made her cringe, but she never wanted to fly tourist again.

Kevin was so relaxed, he snoozed most of the way to Denver. None of their luggage was lost, and Kevin stood for a moment by the carousel, looking around for the sign that would point to the rental car desk.

Megan was thinking that things were going very well when Kevin's cell phone rang.

"Hello?"

Megan pulled the handle up on her rolling luggage and stacked the smaller bag on top. The tiny overnight case perched on top of that one.

Kevin's tone alarmed her.

"What?! When?... How?... Oh, for...! Yes, we just landed. We'll pick up our rental car and drive straight there. Bye."

Megan turned to asked him what was wrong, then yelped with surprise.

A vampire dripping blood from the corner of her mouth stood menacingly behind Kevin. It's yellow eyes glared hatred at Megan.

Kevin looked around when Megan yelped. When he saw the vampire vision, he cried out, "Thank God!" He wrapped his arms around the vampire girl. "Karla! Your mother is frantic!"

Megan marveled at the realism of the girl's costume. She was dressed all in black, and wore a lightweight cape that dangled around her knees. The hem of the cape was uneven and tattered. Her face was painted white except for black eye makeup and black lipstick. Bright red makeup ran in fat drops of blood from one corner of her mouth down her chin. Several of the other passengers in the terminal examined her costume from a safe distance. She was making quite a splash.

Kevin released her from his hug. "How did you get here?" He was already dialing his phone.

"Took the bus." Her voice was schooled in a deep far away tone. "Interesting mode of transportation."

Kevin paused, then spoke into his phone. "Mother? I found her. She came to greet us at the airport…. No, no, call them off. Everything is fine. She's with me. Okay, bye." He put the phone away.

Karla the vampire raised one hand and pointed a finger at Megan. Her nails were two inches long and painted black. Her hands were white, like her face.

"This be your love slave?" Her voice was full of contempt.

Kevin ignored her tone. Instead, he said pleasantly, "Karla, this is Megan. Megan, this is my sister Karla."

Karla hissed at Megan.

Megan thought fast. She could see the love in Kevin's eyes when he looked at his sister. Love and concern. Karla was very important to him, and he was obviously accustomed to her role playing.

In an instant, Megan made her decision. She bowed deeply. "I am unworthy," she said. "I hope to earn your respect over time, Mistress Karla." She maintained her pose, even though she was dying to see Karla's reaction.

Surprise and a hint of pleasure modified Karla's practiced tone, but only slightly. "You may rise, One Called Megan."

Megan straightened up.

Nearby passengers applauded.

Megan fought to keep a straight face.

Karla never broke character, but she waved an arm to acknowledge the crowd. Then she asked Kevin, "Be there a carriage?"

"Yes," said Kevin. "We were just on our way to the rental car desk."

"You may lead the way." She turned her face in Megan's direction without making eye contact. "The One Called Megan may accompany us."

Megan walked with her head down and smiled at the floor.

Chapter Twenty-Eight

KEVIN MARVELED AT MEGAN'S INTUITION. He watched her play into his sister's delusion and wondered if his mother was going to throw a fit. Krystal preferred that everyone ignore Karla's vampire act. But Megan seemed to be enjoying it. When they got to the rental SUV, Kevin used the remote to unlock it and began loading luggage.

Megan gave Karla another mini-bow and asked, "Would Mistress Karla prefer the front seat?"

Karla demurred. "My skin protection formula works well, but I have been out in the daylight far too long. Granted, the tinted windows of the public conveyance shielded me somewhat. However, I would feel much safer ensconced in the middle of the rear seating area."

"As you wish," said Megan. "May I enter the carriage?"

"If you would be so kind as to open the rear door for me. My skin protectant can rub off on other surfaces."

"But of course." Megan opened the rear door and Karla climbed inside. Megan closed the door and caught Kevin's eye. She winked at him, then climbed into the front passenger seat.

Kevin smiled with a shake of his head. This was going to be entertaining. He was delighted that Megan had foiled Karla's attempt to hate her. It had been one of his biggest worries. He couldn't wait to see what happened next.

As they pulled out of the rental lot, Kevin glanced in the rearview mirror. "Karla, are you enjoying the ranch?"

Karla grumbled, but did not respond.

Megan said softly, "Perhaps Mistress Karla needs time to gather her strength. I would think a morning outside the safety of her nest would be exhausting."

Kevin nodded. "Oh. Of course." He glanced sideways at Megan, then turned his face to the window to hide his smile.

Megan faced forward but addressed Karla. "I am honored that you made such a perilous journey to greet us at the airport. I hope to be worthy of your expectations."

In the rearview mirror, Kevin saw Karla nod graciously in response to Megan's words.

Megan continued. "With your permission, Mistress Karla, may we pause in our journey long enough to buy hamburgers and fries?"

Karla leaned her head back against the seat and closed her eyes. A moment later, she growled, "You may."

Once they provisioned themselves, Kevin wondered how Karla would handle eating in front of Megan.

Karla proceeded hesitantly, holding individual fries to her nose to sniff them.

Megan said, "I admire you greatly, Mistress Karla, for adapting to life among humans. You must have spent months adjusting your digestive tract to handle our food."

Karla liked that explanation. "It was a lengthy process," she intoned, then popped a fry into her mouth.

The rest of the trip to the ranch went quickly.

"Only another twenty minutes," said Kevin. "I think you'll enjoy the ranch."

"Wonderful," said Megan. "I do love the outdoors."

Karla growled.

Megan added respectfully, "Especially when it allows me to run errands for Mistress Karla so she can remain safely out of the sunlight."

Karla made an approving mew.

. When they turned onto the blacktop road and drove under the arched sign for the Rocking Eagle Ranch, Karla surprised Kevin by leaning forward.

"One Called Megan," she intoned, "I grow fond of you. Therefore I offer this warning. Beware the sorceress known as Krystal. She means well, but she often wreaks havoc." She leaned back in her seat.

Megan's brows went up. "Is this sorceress your enemy, Mistress Karla?"

"Only unintentionally. My true enemy dwells within the Chamber of Gold. He wagers for a living."

Kevin translated, "Dad plays the stock market. The Chamber of Gold—"

Megan interrupted, "Forgive me, Lord Kevin, but Mistress Karla does speak clearly."

Kevin wasn't certain but he thought he heard a giggle of delight from the back seat. He smiled and kept driving.

Megan continued. "Mistress Karla, may I ask a question?"

"You may."

"I notice that Lord Kevin has hazel eyes, but yours are a magnificent yellow. Are they your birth color, or did they change when you turned?"

Kevin tried to interpret Megan's question for himself.

Karla made a contented sound. "My eyes changed when I turned," she said with dignity.

Kevin nodded to himself. When Karla took on her vampire persona, she used her allowance to purchase yellow contact lenses. No matter what Krystal did, Karla was never without replacements. They would search her room endlessly, and more than once Karla emailed him that they'd held her under the shower and washed them out of her eyes. But every morning, she reemerged with a fresh set of yellow contacts.

Megan said, "Thank you, Mistress Karla. I must say, they are truly awe inspiring."

Kevin checked his rear view mirror and his heart leaped.

Karla was smiling.

Chapter Twenty-Nine

BY THE TIME THEY PULLED into the long circular driveway in front of the main house, Karla's smile was gone.

Megan's eyes widened with delight as she drank in her surroundings. "It's three stories high! White clapboard, and a wrap around porch, and gingerbread! You have acorn finials! Oh, my God, I'm in heaven."

Two workers in painters' overalls were busy with maintenance, painting the newel posts on the porch.

A middle-aged woman used the handrail to descend the steps carefully. Megan's first impression told her the woman was an invalid.

"Mom," said Kevin fondly.

"Krystal," hissed Karla.

Kevin put the SUV in park and turned off the engine. "I'll give her a hand." He slipped out of the car and went to his mother's side.

"She will disrespect me," said Karla. "Pay her no mind."

Megan nodded, then got out of the car and went round to open Karla's door.

Krystal's features were drawn. Megan couldn't tell if she was angry or in pain. Perhaps both.

"Karla! You had me worried sick! I had to call the authorities."

Megan looked around. None were in evidence.

Karla whirled her cape over her head and hissed at her mother as she ran up the stairs into the house.

Kevin gave Krystal a gentle hug. "It's good to see you, mom. You look better than I expected. Your new medication must be working."

"I have good days and bad days," said Krystal stiffly. She eyed Megan up and down. "This is your bride?"

Kevin nodded. "Mom, this is Megan. Megan, this is my mother, Krystal Fineman Wake."

Megan held out a hand. "So nice to meet you, Mrs. Wake."

"Please, call me Krystal."

Megan smiled but doubted she could call this woman anything but Mrs. Wake. She noticed that although Mrs. Wake appeared fragile, her gray eyes were hard as steel.

An eight-year-old boy stumbled against the screen door as he emerged from the house. His gaze was fixed on his iPad. "Krystal! Krystal!"

Krystal cringed. "I'm right here, Keegan. No need to shout."

He was thumping his finger against the screen of his device. "My battery needs charging. I can't do nothing!"

"Anything," said Krystal. "You can't do anything."

"That's what I said," pouted Keegan. He glanced up at Kevin. "About time you got here. Everyone is crazy."

Kevin ruffled Keegan's dark hair. "I missed you, too."

"Likely story." The boy fastened his dark brown eyes on Megan. They lit up. "Is she a movie star? Are you going to marry a movie star?"

"No, she's not a movie star, and yes, she is my bride."

Keegan wasn't sure how to take the mixed answer. "You're pretty," he said at last, "but I was hoping for someone famous."

"Sorry to disappoint," said Megan. She held out a hand. "Nice to meet you."

Keegan snubbed her and headed inside, calling over his shoulder, "I have to recharge! I'll be in my room, Krystal!"

"Kids," said Kevin.

"He's quite the electronic wizard," said Krystal. "Although I was hoping a summer on the ranch would inspire him to spend some time outdoors."

"Why does he call you Krystal?"

"It's my name." Krystal seemed surprised by the question.

"But you're his mother."

"Names are important."

Megan could've sworn that Krystal's nose tipped upward as she spoke those words.

Kevin said, "Mom, let me help you inside. Megan, you've met the siblings. Would you like a tour of the ranch?"

"Could I lie down for half an hour first?" said Megan. One hand rubbed her thigh.

"Of course."

"How thoughtless of me," said Krystal. "Kevin, she's in the blue room. Something old, something new," she recited.

Megan finished with a smile, "Something borrowed, something blue. Thank you. I look forward to seeing more of this spectacular home."

A flush of pleasure colored Krystal's cheeks. "You like the Victorian motif?"

"It's glorious," said Megan. "Just like the house I pinned on my bedroom wall as a child."

Chapter Thirty

KEVIN TOOK THE LUGGAGE inside and carried Megan's upstairs for her. By the time they got to the blue room, she looked very tired.

"I'll be all right," she said. "I just need a short rest."

"It has been a very long day. It's almost three-thirty. Dinner is early here. Ranch time. Cookie serves around five, so you've got time to put your feet up."

"Thanks."

Kevin headed back downstairs for a private word with his mother. He found her in the formal sitting room at the front of the house. He glanced about the room and paid more attention to detail than he'd ever done before. Megan loved the Victorian decor. She would adore this room.

Krystal was seated in a wing chair by the front window. A tea tray perched on the little table by the chair.

Kevin pulled a footstool close and sat at his mother's knee.

"Oh, darling, I love when you do that." Krystal gave him a tiny smile. "Tea?"

"No, I'm fine."

Krystal poured her own. "Tell me, Kev. What's wrong with her?"

Kevin frowned. "Nothing. She's perfect. I thought you'd like her!"

"Oh, don't get me wrong. She was still in the car after Karla showed up at the airport. I'm certain she'll do. I asked what's wrong with her. Something with her thigh?"

"Oh, that." Leave it to his mother to pick up on the smallest physical ailment. "She was in a car crash six months ago. She had a broken femur and months of infections. She just got out of the hospital a few days ago."

Krystal eyed him sternly. "Is she strong enough to stand up to your father?"

Kevin shrugged. "I'm not putting her in the ring with him, you know. I think she's pretty strong. And you should have seen her with Karla! It was incredible. She even got Karla to smile."

Krystal's eyes widened. "I don't believe it. Karla didn't say anything about a smile."

It was Kevin's turn to pin his mother with a glare. "Did you set that up? Did you send Karla to the airport?!"

Krystal's brows rose and she schooled her expression. "No! She frightened me out of my wits by running off to meet you. I merely suggested that she might have an opportunity to earn back some privileges if she gave me a two-minute summary of the meeting. She only left a few seconds before you came in." Her lips curled in a tiny smile. "She told me her first impression of Megan was quite a good one. She said she'll do."

"Well, that's good. But what kind of privileges are you restoring? I thought you grounded her for six months and took her phone away."

"That was just during her…" Krystal paused to choose her words carefully. "Her hospitalization. Her therapist felt the outside world was a distraction. And when she came home, she seemed to have lost some of the old spark. She didn't battle her father for phone privileges at all. That worried me more than anything. Just as well. He destroyed her phone with a hammer."

"Did they medicate her?" Kevin's brow darkened.

"Not to my knowledge. But it was a rigorous program." She sipped tea and set it aside. "Frankly, Kevin, they told me they wouldn't take her back. They said her steadfast delusion in the face of all their efforts was a disruption for the other patients. They told me if we had further concerns, we should choose a different facility."

"They gave up," said Kevin abruptly. "Those money-grubbing bastards."

"On the bright side, your sister seemed pleased to be home again. She continues to wear her yellow contact lenses, but I've decided to choose my battles."

"And dad?"

Krystal dismissed her husband with a wave of her hand. "I think he has become part of the problem. Ever since we came here, Karla has been... well, not participatory, but at least more willing to avoid conflict."

"What exactly does that mean?"

Krystal shrugged. "She doesn't run after the help screaming like a vampire anymore. I find that a refreshing step in the right direction."

Kevin laughed out loud. "Who did she chase?"

"Mr. Garcia's wife, Rosalinda." She rolled her eyes. "You should have seen her face! Priceless. Karla tried the same trick on Cookie, but it backfired."

"I can imagine."

"Yes. Cookie picked up a cast iron pan and screamed right back at her. To hear Cookie tell it, Karla bowed down to her and christened her the Queen of the Clutch. No outbursts since that day, thank goodness."

Kevin chuckled. "Well, you know how I feel."

"Yes. You think it's a phase. I hope you're right. Your father is investigating prices on some very stern Swiss schools."

"Oh, you're not going to seriously consider sending her away, are you?"

"When your father gets a bee in his bonnet, retreat is the safest strategy. That's why you're getting married in Colorado instead of New York."

"About that," said Kevin. But he was cut short by a knock at the door of the parlor.

"Is this a private party?"

"Zach!" Kevin stood up and embraced the ranch foreman. "It's great to see you. Hey, you've finally succeeded in tanning your tough old hide to match your chestnut gelding. And is that gray hair?"

"Smart aleck. You got a lot of nerve, noticing my gray, when you ain't been around for years."

Krystal smiled softly. "You tell him, Zachary. I had to organize a wedding to get him back here."

Zach's eyes softened when he looked at Krystal. "Well worth it, ma'am. And just in time." He handed her a folded letter. "This came in the morning mail."

Krystal opened it and scanned it quickly. Then she crumpled it in her fist and threw it. "Oh, that man! Will he never stop?!"

Chapter Thirty-One

MEGAN LET HERSELF DOZE on top of the quilt. She didn't want to close her eyes because the room was filled with beautiful things and she was trying to catalogue them all in her memory. But her body demanded rest, so she dozed.

She wasn't sure how much time had passed when there was a soft rapping at the door.

"Come in."

Karla entered. She had washed the makeup off her face and hands but was still wearing the same clothes.

"Are you sleeping?" Her non-vampire voice was a pleasant contralto.

Megan's brows met in a tiny frown. "I'm not sure."

"I can come back."

"No, no. Please. Come in." She patted the bed for Karla to come sit.

Karla settled carefully next to her. "Thanks for not freaking out at the airport."

Megan shook off the cobwebs of her nap. "No problem. You were amazing."

"Really?" Karla brightened.

"Did you travel all the way from the ranch in costume?"

"Nah. I wore the cape as a sash and I didn't put my face paint on until I got to the airport. I'd like to wear it all the time, but I break out." She crossed her eyes then relaxed them.

Megan smiled. "So underneath the bleak vampire act, you are a comedian."

"Shhh. You mustn't tell the parents that it's all an act. If they find out, they'll never pay any attention to me at all. Krystal is already trying to ignore me. She thinks if she doesn't react in any way, I'll leave the Undead and rejoin the stupid boring Living."

"My lips are sealed, Mistress Karla."

"Cool. So, did you and Kevin do it yet?"

"Do it? Oh! No. I was raised to not do it until I was married, and—"

"Wow. So old Kev's got a bride who can really wear white."

Megan asked uncertainly, "Do you think I'm a dork?"

"No way. Lots of girls at my school take pledges not to do it before marriage. It's the in thing."

"Excellent. What are you wearing to the wedding?"

Karla rolled her eyes and stood up to go. "Here we go again. See ya."

"Wait! What did I say?"

Karla paused, her hand on the door knob. "Mother has already told me I can't attend as myself, so I will be in my room for the duration."

"What? I don't get it."

Karla leaned against the door and crossed her arms. "Krystal said I can't come as a vampire. So I'm not coming."

"Oh, no!" Megan sat up. "No, please, I want you there. As yourself."

Karla gave her a what-are-you-talking-about look. "As a vampire?"

"Yes! Can you just imagine the wedding pictures?! It will be awesome! And you are so talented with your makeup. I want you there, hissing at the photographer and crouching in the background. Everything!"

Karla's eyes shot heavenward. "You *do* exist! You answered my prayers!" Even though she spoke with sarcasm, the joy in her heart was all too evident. "Thanks, Megan." She rushed to the bed and bent to give Megan a hug. "I'll cook up something super special!"

"I can't wait."

"I gotta go. I want to be at the dinner table in full regalia. I owe it to Queen Cookie of Culinaria."

She flew out the door.

Megan chuckled to herself. Why did parents always overreact? She wondered if Karla's school offered drama classes. The girl was a natural, and she was truly gifted as a makeup artist.

She tried to remember what her own life was like at fourteen. She cringed at the memory. Walking around with her eyes on the floor, shoulders hunched forward to hide her new bosoms. When she had to stand in front of her English class and recite a poem, she actually fainted! It took years to live that down. Her admiration for the dramatic Karla rose even higher. How creative to invent a different persona, one with power, a fearless vampire to deal with the life of a fourteen-year-old. Overall, she still had the same problems that Megan had at fourteen, but she was attacking them in a very different manner.

As she freshened up for dinner, she couldn't help but smile at the thought of the wedding photos she and Karla would create.

Chapter Thirty-Two

KEVIN RETRIEVED THE CRUMPLED letter from the corner where Krystal had flung it.

"What's going on, Zach? What's this all about?"

Zach hooked his thumbs over his belt. "Your father wants me to make room in my schedule next week for a team of surveyors to come out and break up the property into parcels for sale."

"He can't do that! He doesn't own this property."

Krystal breathed through flared nostrils. Her words came with difficulty. "He'll never stop! That's why, that's why—"

"She needs her medication." Zach stepped to the door and called, "Cookie!" A moment later, he returned with an inhaler. "Here you go, ma'am."

Krystal used the inhaler and sank back on her seat cushion, her eyes closed. After a few quiet moments, she spoke softly.

"That is why I called you when I did, Kevin. He has wagered with his Wall Street buddies that he will own this property the day after your birthday, and he has flaunted his disregard for my family history and any attachment I might have to all things Fineman."

"It's stupid to sell the ranch in parcels," said Kevin. "It's plain stupid to sell the ranch, period. I was hoping our lawyers would find a way out of this marriage requirement."

"They said they stand very little chance in court because my parents set it up as an irrevocable trust. Besides, if a judgment came down in our favor, your father would use that in his own battle to defy the letter of the trust to take over everything I brought to the marriage and add cash to his foreign coffers. Off-shore bank accounts indeed." She spat the phrase. Then she sat up and gathered herself together. "Have you warned your young bride about your father? He might try something before the wedding day."

Kevin looked grim. "I think he already has. He had someone spying on us with binoculars."

"The venomous old fart."

"Mother!" Kevin shook his head and chuckled. "I don't know how you've put up with him all these years."

"What? Me, leave? And violate that ironclad prenup he insisted on? Lose everything that might possibly come to my children, out of spite for their father? Humph. I'm tougher than that. And I won't let him win. Friday we will have a wedding right here in this room. That will secure your inheritance. And Monday, the lawyers will file the necessary papers, delivering the trust into your hands." All the color suddenly dropped out of her face. She grabbed Kevin. "The license! The marriage license!"

Kevin patted her arm. "All taken care of."

Krystal slumped in relief. "All right, then. Now if your sweet young bride can survive the week, everything should work out." She leaned against the back of the chair and let her head tip sideways against the wing. "Now let me rest for a few minutes before dinner, if you don't mind."

"Sure, mom." Kevin left the room with Zach. Outside, he asked, "How is she really?"

"About the same. The stress of dealing with your father has taken its toll. But let me tell you, hearing you were on your way and you'd found a bride? Well, she has been much better since that phone call."

"And the kids?"

Zach looked grim. "You saw your sister. Still into the vampire thing. Keegan? Well, your mother is too exhausted to tackle his addiction to computer games. He just sits around the house, glued to that danged tablet. He was so disappointed the first day they arrived, because Buttercup wasn't available for fun and games. She's getting older, and she's got a lot on her plate right now. She's staying out at the office with me during the day."

"He's not interested in the horses?"

"He came out to look, but he's afraid of them. They're too big, and he doesn't have the upbringing you did. You better get out to the barn and say hello to Honey. That mare knew the minute you drove up, and she is having a fit."

Kevin grinned. "Let's go, then. We've got time before dinner."

Chapter Thirty-Three

DINNER WAS SERVED IN THE FAMILY DINING ROOM.

Krystal stuck to her plan of ignoring Karla. The result was an immensely entertaining meal. The teen stalked Kevin, hissed at Queen Cookie every time she entered the room, and made a huge show of sniffing her baby brother.

Keegan was used to it. He pulled a piece of garlic out of his shirt pocket and rubbed it on his head. "Stay back, creature of the night," he said, as simply as one would say, "Pass the salt."

Karla's reaction was worthy of Bela Lugosi.

Once dinner was served, Karla slipped into a chair next to Megan and began to eat with apparent gusto.

Krystal froze with her wine glass half way to her lips.

"Karla! You're eating." Every syllable full of hope.

Karla remained in character, using her vampire voice. "I have worked very hard for many months to adjust my digestive system to human food. I do what I must to survive."

Kevin and Megan hid smiles behind their napkins. Karla had quoted Megan's explanation almost word for word.

"I see," said Krystal. "Very well. Bon appetit."

Karla growled.

Krystal ignored her. "Pass the mashed potatoes, Kevin."

Megan finished her roast beef and was on her second serving of

130

mixed vegetables and potatoes when Krystal turned a schooled face to her. "Please tell us a little about yourself, my dear."

Cookie moved efficiently, bringing trays of food, removing dirtied plates. She looked like somebody's grandmother, with steel gray hair swept back and covered with an old chef's hat. She was stocky, but gave the impression of strength, not excess weight. Her cheeks were pink and her pale eyes twinkled with humor.

Megan began by lifting her water glass in Cookie's direction. "First of all, I'd like to thank Cookie for a wonderful meal. It's all so delicious."

Cookie seemed surprised and delighted at the same time. "You're most welcome." She winked at Megan and went about her business.

Krystal cleared her throat.

Megan took the hint. "Well, I grew up in northern California. My dad was a preacher and he had little churches in Cloverdale, Ukiah, and Willits. My mom stayed at home mostly. It was a full time job, making ends meet. We bounced around wherever the most parishioners showed up. I went to school at UC Davis."

"What did you study?"

"Social Services. I was on my way to Seattle to start my first job at a community center there when my car was hit by a logging truck. The driver fell asleep at the wheel, and I ended up in the hospital for six months. The people at the community center were very sympathetic but had to hire someone else after three months. They were willing to keep me on a list, though." She shrugged. "I hadn't heard anything else from them up to the time I met Kevin."

"Where are your parents now?" asked Karla. Then, in vampire voice, "I mean, where do thy parents dwell?"

"They're in Central America. Dad wanted to build a mission." Her voice faltered. "I assume they're still there. I can't seem to reach them."

Megan was surprised by the kindness in Krystal's tone as she said, "I'm sure they are quite all right, my dear."

"Thanks. I hope so."

Megan saw Krystal shoot Kevin a glance, but she let it go. This family had way too many quirks for a simple over-the-table glance to count for anything.

Keegan was staring into his lap.

Megan asked, "You okay, Keegan?"

Krystal's tone sharpened. "Put that tablet away or I will smash it against a wall!"

"No!" Keegan jumped off his chair and ran out of the room, clutching his iPad to his chest.

Karla rolled her eyes. "Good one, Krystal. Superb parenting."

Krystal glared at her daughter.

Megan forced a smile. "Too bad he doesn't love the outdoors like his brother."

Krystal and Karla broke off their glare fest and looked a question at Kevin.

Megan blinked. "You know. His summer job as a lumberjack."

"Lumberjack?!" Krystal was horrified.

Karla was not. "Cool!"

Kevin dabbed at his lips with his napkin. "Mom, you said you knew all about what I was doing in Seattle."

"I didn't know you were risking your life running up and down mountains and dodging falling trees."

Kevin kept it light. "It seemed like a better idea than paying a gym membership."

Karla suppressed a smile. "He be buff," she intoned.

Cookie served coffee and carrot cake. She leaned over Megan's shoulder. "My own recipe. Cream cheese frosting."

The carrot cake was so delicious, no one did much talking. When Krystal stood and excused herself after dinner, Kevin rose as well.

Megan got up. "I'm just going to help Cookie with the dishes."

Krystal's eyes widened, but she said nothing.

Karla said, "The Undead do not do dishes." She escaped to her room.

Megan slipped into the kitchen. "Cookie, how can I help?"

Cookie peeked into the dining room to make sure everyone had left. Then she handed Megan a plate with a generous square of carrot cake on it.

"Would you mind taking this upstairs to little Keegan?"

Megan found his room easily enough. It was the one with the action hero posters. The door was ajar.

"Knock, knock," she said softly, pushing the door all the way open.

"I'm busy," said Keegan with as much authority as an eight-year-old could muster.

"Cookie sent contraband." Megan closed the door behind her.

Keegan looked up from a computer screen, and his eyes grew big. "Yes! Cookie loves me!"

Megan smiled as he dug into the carrot cake. Even with a fork and the napkin she'd brought, he got more frosting on his face than in his mouth.

"You need a mechanical napkin," said Megan. "You know, like a Transformer that knows which part of your face to clean."

"Good idea. You want some?" He held up the demolished cake and offered his fork.

"Thanks, but no. I ate my piece downstairs." She tilted her head to glimpse his computer screen. "What are you working on?"

"Feeding my dog."

"On a computer?"

"It's an avatar."

"Wow. When I was your age, I didn't know what that was."

"When you were my age, they didn't exist."

Megan laughed. "You're funny!"

Keegan rubbed the napkin across his mouth. "Krystal says I'm rude."

"You really know a lot about computers, don't you?"

Keegan nodded eagerly. "But my dog keeps dying."

"Oh, no!"

"I forget to boot the program. I have to feed him and give him water and walk him. All on the computer. Today he chewed up my sofa. See?" He turned the screen so she could see that the cartoon dog had indeed destroyed the cartoon sofa on the screen.

"He looks skinny."

"I forgot to feed him again."

"But you carry your iPad everywhere. Just feed him from the iPad."

"Can't. It's an old program and I only have it on my computer. The iPad is too new for it. Krystal says I don't need anymore games this summer. So I have to wait."

Megan sat on the edge of Keegan's bed. "Kevin says you're a computer genius."

Keegan shook his head. "Not really. I just know more than anybody else in the family. I'm not that smart at school."

"Oh, I find that hard to believe. I'll bet you're doing really well. What's your favorite subject?"

"Recess." Keegan blew a raspberry. Then he said, "Math, I guess. But I like to read, too. And I love animal studies, but social studies is boring."

"For a guy who loves animal studies, you seem to spend a lot of time with computers. Why not go out and study the ranch animals?"

"Are you kidding? They're huge." He rolled his eyes. "My favorite was Buttercup, but Zach said she can't come out and play right now."

"Buttercup?"

"She's Zach's yellow Lab." Keegan's face got wistful. "I love that dog." His expression darkened. "Dad won't let me have a dog in the apartment. He says they pee on the carpets. He doesn't like dogs." He turned and asked, "How can anyone not like dogs?!"

"I don't know, Keegan. That's a mystery to me, too. But I know how you feel. My father never wanted a dog in the house either. My mother snuck in a kitten, but we knew he'd throw a fit if we tried to get a puppy." She sighed heavily. "I really want a dog."

"Me, too," said Keegan.

Chapter Thirty-Four

MEGAN LEFT KEEGAN TO HIS animated pet and went looking for Kevin. She found him on the front porch in the swing.

"Room for two?"

Kevin smiled up at her. "Definitely. I was just wondering if I was going to have to take a ticket for a chance to talk to you."

Megan sat down.

Kevin took her hand in his, and Megan felt a zing of electricity, just like at Lake Tahoe the day before, and at Pike's Market. He was so darned good looking!

"Your brother and your sister are priceless."

"Thanks. I can't tell you how relieved I am to hear you say that!"

Megan held her hand out palm down and wiggled it back and forth. "Your mother? Mmmm, jury's still out."

"Speaking of parents," said Kevin, "my old man is up to his usual chicanery. He sent Zach a letter, telling him to make time in his schedule to meet with surveyors. Dad is acting like the ranch is his already and he's planning to sell it."

"Two questions," said Megan. "First, is this the Zach you mentioned on the plane?"

"Yes, our ranch foreman. He and mom grew up together. You'll meet him tomorrow."

"Okay. And second, your dad doesn't stand a chance, does he? I mean, with the way things have played out..." She left it hanging.

"Theoretically, no. But he is notorious for rocking the boat at the last minute. Mom thinks he'll be scheming to the very end."

"Well, he knows about me. We saw his spy in Tahoe. Did you tell your mom about that?"

"Yes."

"And about Reno?"

Kevin squeezed her hand. "I keep trying, but we keep getting interrupted. By the way, mom wanted to know if you're strong enough to deal with all this craziness."

"So far, so good. What's on the schedule for tomorrow?"

Krystal's voice cut through the twilight. "I have arranged for my personal seamstress to spend the morning fitting your wedding gown."

Megan started to pull her hand back, but Kevin wouldn't let it go.

Krystal settled in a wicker rocker a few feet away. "Young lady, you have made a very good impression with two people who are not easy to impress. Both Karla and Keegan give you two thumbs up."

Megan smiled. "I like them, too."

Krystal hummed with amusement. "You are a gift from above. Oh! Have you met my foreman? Zach? Zachary!"

Megan recognized Zach as the man on the computer screen when she'd done a Google search on Kevin's family. He looked a bit older than in the photo, and his hair was very gray at the temples. But he was dressed like a ranch hand and wearing cowboy boots, just like in the photo.

More interesting, however, was the transformation that came over Krystal when Zach joined them on the porch.

Krystal's voice softened. "Zachary King, this is Megan—"

"Mully," supplied Kevin.

"Megan Mully, Kevin's fiancée. After the wedding on Friday, Megan will be giving the orders around here. Try to make a good impression."

Megan's mouth dropped open at Krystal's pronouncement, but she closed it quickly as Zach stepped close and offered his hand.

"It's a pleasure, little lady."

Megan shook his hand and wondered if he'd call her 'little lady' if she was standing up. But she smiled and replied, "From what I've seen so far, you're doing a great job. Do you have a dog named Buttercup?"

Zach stepped back. "Why, yes. How'd you know that?"

"Keegan told me. He misses her a lot."

"She's six years old, and when I rescued her four years ago, I was told she was fixed. But lo and behold, she had herself a litter of pups. Three have gone to homes, but there's two left, and believe me, she has had enough of motherhood."

"Two? That's perfect!" She turned to Kevin. "Guess what I want for a wedding present!"

Kevin shot a questioning glance at Zach.

"No problem here," said Zach. "I was hoping we'd get to keep a couple at the ranch. But let me get their final puppy shots tomorrow. You can take possession the day after. If Krystal doesn't object." He raised his brows and addressed the last sentence to Krystal.

"Megan will be the lady of the house, so if she wants a puppy, she shall have a puppy. And you're right about the timing. She'll be much too busy with her dress tomorrow to add a new family member."

Zach held a hand out to Krystal. "Ma,am? May I interest you in a stroll through the orchard?"

"Why, yes, you may." Krystal took his hand and let him help her out of the rocker. "Megan, the seamstress will expect you in the parlor at nine a.m."

"Yes, ma'am," said Megan. She watched Krystal walk away on Zach's arm. When they were out of earshot, she tapped Kevin's arm.

"Did you see that?! Did you see?"

"See what?"

"How could you not see it?" She lowered her voice. "Your mother is in love with Zachary King."

Chapter Thirty-Five

Wednesday, June 27

MEGAN DISCOVERED THAT Krystal expected her to sleep separately from Kevin since the wedding hadn't taken place yet. At first, she was relieved. Then she was disappointed. When she signed their prenup, she was certain this was just a job. But now, she found herself growing fonder of Kevin every hour. And he appeared more attractive than ever as she witnessed his affection for his family. She allowed herself a fanciful moment, imagining him knocking softly on her door after everyone else was asleep. Then she blushed hotly. His mother's room was right next door! She couldn't imagine spending their first intimate night next door to his mother.

She slept like a baby in the blue room. When she opened her eyes, it was already eight o'clock. She rushed through her shower, got dressed, and headed downstairs to the kitchen, looking for coffee. The house was very quiet.

Cookie was ready for her. She poured her a big mug of coffee and offered her a plate of toast.

"Thank you, Cookie. Morning, Keegan."

Keegan did not look up. His thumbs were moving furiously over the controls of an electronic game. "Morning."

"Where is everyone?"

Cookie poured herself a cup of coffee and joined Megan and Keegan at the table. "Kevin and Krystal went riding about seven. Karla is still asleep, most likely. She is a teenager, after all. I just got back from taking coffee and rolls over to the office yonder."

"That big metal building over there?"

"That's where the ranch business is done. It takes a lot to run a place like this."

"Speaking of which," said Megan, "last night Krystal said that after the wedding on Friday, I will be the lady of the house."

Cookie drew inward and started to get up from the table. "Yes, ma'am."

"No, no, please sit! I was surprised by her announcement. Surely she will always be the lady of the house, not me."

Cookie relaxed and reached for a slice of toast. "Oh, that. Yes, in a way she'll always be head of this household. But she's been waiting for years for Kevin to get married so he can inherit the place, take over the trust, and run the ranch. And his wife will legally be the lady of the house. Mrs. Krystal's parents wrote that into the trust. They never figured that their male heirs would die before the property could be transferred. They never made arrangements for a female heir, except that she could hold the property and the estate for safekeeping until her son was old enough to inherit. And then, of course, there was the famous marriage requirement. Kevin has to marry before his twenty-fifth birthday, or the property and the estate both go to Mrs. Krystal, which she deserves, but she's afraid her husband will get his hands on it if that happens." Her inflection on the word "husband" told Megan how she felt about that idea.

"Wow. That's barbaric."

"It's very Victorian," said Cookie. "They didn't figure a woman could run a place like this. Mrs. Krystal is a trustee, but Zach is really in charge of the ranch. But of course, he defers to Mrs. Krystal."

"And Mr. Wake never tried to install his own man as foreman?"

Cookie threw her head back and laughed. "You are a very bright young lady. As a matter of fact, he has tried, three times that I know of. But the biggest power Mrs. Krystal has is being able to choose her foreman."

"That poor woman."

"Well, she has a lot upstairs herself. She got you and Kevin here for a wedding, didn't she?" She picked up a napkin and reached over to wipe peanut butter off Keegan's face. "Mr. Keegan, please don't leave the table with peanut butter smeared all over your face and fingers."

"Okay." Without looking up, he grabbed the napkin and smeared the peanut butter over a wider swath than before.

Cookie shook her head in mock disgust. "I'd better get a wash cloth. And you, Miss Megan, eat your toast. You have a full morning of fittings ahead of you. Mrs. Krystal's seamstress is a perfectionist."

Three hours later, Megan decided that Cookie's definition of perfectionist matched other people's definition of sadist. Her leg throbbed from spending most of the morning standing up as Genevieve's fingers flew, tugging here, loosening there, hemming, trimming, and stitching away. At last, Megan begged for mercy.

"Maybe we can continue later," she said. "I'm recovering from a traumatic injury, and I simply cannot stand here any longer." She moved toward a chair.

"Don't sit! This dress is not for sitting!" Genevieve straightened up and cracked her back. "No one told me you were convalescing. Let me help you out of that dress. I can finish the rest on the dummy." She patted Megan's arm. "You've been an absolute dream to work with. And you'll be a gorgeous bride."

As Megan left the parlor, she decided she needed to be more open about her injury. She could have saved herself at least an hour of torture by speaking up earlier.

She found herself heading for the kitchen again, not for food or coffee, but for Cookie's comforting presence. She no sooner entered from the dining room when a stern, blond man with angry green eyes came through the back door.

"Who the hell are you!?" he bellowed. "Where is everybody? Are you the trollop my son is trying to pass off as a legitimate bride? I saw the pictures of you two swilling champagne on the beach at Lake Tahoe. Get out! Get out of my house!"

Megan had thought she was strong enough to face him down, but he reminded her so much of her own father in a temper that she turned and ran, just like she used to do as a child.

Chapter Thirty-Six

KEVIN FOUND MEGAN IN HER ROOM, face pressed into her pillow. When he touched her shoulder, she jumped.

"Oh, Kevin! Your father is worse than mine. What a horrid beast of a man. You win again." She tried to make a joke, but her tears garbled the sound.

Kevin pulled her close. "He's such a jerk," he grumbled. "He's getting an earful from Krystal right now."

"I should have stood up to him! He made me feel like a helpless little girl again. And I'm really pissed about that. I'm going down there right now, and tell him this isn't his house. It stopped being his house yesterday." She tried to pull free, but Kevin held tight.

"Let's not rush," he said. "We don't want him to be forewarned. There are still a couple of days for him to come up with strategies. I would rather have him cracking the whip over the backs of his lawyers than turning his rage on you."

Relieved, Megan slumped against him. "Okay. Thanks." She took a breath and realized that Kevin's manly scent was more than comforting. It was also stirring feelings deep inside. Not only was he devastatingly handsome and buff, but she'd realized since arriving that he was giving up his life of freedom in Seattle for the good of his crazy, funny, attention-deprived siblings. At that moment, Megan was filled with love for him.

But she still didn't want to get intimate next door to his mother's bedroom, even if he were so inclined. There it was again, that twinge of disappointment.

"Let's take a break," said Kevin. "Let's go into town for a while. I'll buy you lunch."

"That sounds great," said Megan, hastily wiping her eyes. "Let me run a brush through my hair."

"I'll be standing guard right outside your door." He planted a kiss on her cheek.

Leaving the ranch for a few hours was a huge relief. Kevin drove the battered old pickup as if he were in it every day.

Hanging onto the dash, Megan said, "I thought we'd be taking the rental car."

Kevin laughed. "Zach and one of the hands had to go into Eagle's Toe this morning so they dropped the rental off while they were there. No point paying for it if we don't need it. I learned to drive in this truck. It's more fun than the rental anyway. Zach said if I could drive this baby, I could drive anything."

"Zach taught you to drive?"

"Yep. He's trying to coax Karla behind the wheel as well. I think she needs one more year, and then she'll jump at the opportunity."

"They're great kids," said Megan. "Oh, look! A toy store! We have to go in. I want to get the kids a surprise."

Kevin watched as Megan kept adding to the stash of toys in her cart. Outdoor chalk, several cars and trucks, a dump truck, and a road grader. She even picked up a few action figures, including Hollywood's most recent action heroes and some soldiers. Then she went down the aisle for costumes and theatrical makeup. She included a book on the artistry of stage makeup. Then she found an aisle with Halloween props.

"Karla has to have a skull that lights up, don't you think?"

Kevin scratched his head. "I'm impressed with your insight, but don't you think Keegan would like one of those new electronic games?"

Megan pinned him with a look. "He already sneaks those things to the table and never goes outside. I'm getting him toys he can appreciate at the ranch. He needs a sandbox, by the way. A big one, so he can play with his dump truck."

"And Karla needs more face paint?"

"She's very talented! Who knows what she will become next. I'm just encouraging her strengths. And besides, she'll need all of this to do our makeup for the second set of wedding photos."

Kevin's face screwed into a question. "What are you talking about?"

Megan pushed the cart toward the checkout. "Your mother told her she couldn't come to the wedding as a vampire. Since it's my wedding, I told her she could. I hope Krystal understands, but either way I want Karla in the wedding photos, and if she wants to be a vampire, I told her to camp it up. Do some poses. And I thought it would be great fun if we keep the photographer around and let her do our makeup afterward, so we can have a whole group picture of a vampire wedding! Don't you think that would be fun?"

Kevin was speechless.

"It would go a long way to bringing Karla out of her isolation," said Megan.

Kevin tilted his head to one side. "You know, I think it could work. All right, I'm in." He pulled out his credit card.

"No, wait. These are my gifts to the kids." She took her wallet out of her purse. "Allow me the illusion of using my own money."

Kevin slipped an arm around her and squeezed her gently. "I don't mean to destroy your illusion, but as of day before yesterday, this *is* your money."

Megan paused, thought for a moment, then tucked her wallet away. She took the credit card out of his hand and said lightly, "That's right! Thanks, honey." With a big smile, she handed the card to the cashier.

She did use her cash at the little restaurant where they stopped for lunch. She couldn't let Kevin use his credit card for everything.

"You know how I feel about credit cards and debt." Her hand clutched her purse as she spoke.

"As soon as I inherit," said Kevin, interpreting her concern, "I'll pay off those medical bills. Don't worry."

Megan made a face. "You can already read my mind?"

"Of course. We've known each other a whole five days. Plenty of time for mind reading."

The gifts were a big hit.

Karla growled, "Thank you, One Called Megan." She already had the book open as she climbed the stairs.

Keegan raised his action figures in the air. "My favorites! How did you know?"

Kevin said, "Bro, they're plastered all over your door."

"Oh, right. Look, they fit in the trucks! Come on!"

Megan and Kevin helped him carry his trucks and action figures outside.

"We need dirt," said Keegan.

"The horseshoe pit," said Kevin. "It's filled with sand. How's that?"

"Perfect!" Keegan ran ahead, and plopped down in the sand, already pushing it around with his grader.

Megan lowered herself carefully to the ground and began placing action figures inside vehicles. "Build me some roads," she said, "so these guys will have places to go."

Kevin knelt beside her on one knee and began scooping dirt with the dump truck. He winked at her and mouthed the word, "Brilliant."

Megan tapped her temple with one finger and mouthed back, "Genius." Then she glanced around them. "Umm, I didn't see your father inside. And I don't see any other vehicles. Did he leave?"

Krystal's voice came from behind her.

"Unfortunately, no. Douglas went into town to meet with his lawyers. They're staying at a hotel there."

Megan turned. "Oh, hi, Krystal. I couldn't resist buying some gifts for Keegan and Karla."

Krystal's expression remained stern, but her eyes softened. "So I see. Did they teach you this in college?"

Megan shrugged. "My concentration was in Youth Development, so in a way, yes."

"Hmph." Krystal watched her youngest crawling through the sand, building roads with on-ramps and off-ramps. "What do you know," she said. "Well, well. Please see to it that he cleans up before dinner."

Megan nodded. "I will."

One corner of Krystal's mouth turned up. "And you, too." She turned and moved carefully toward the house.

Kevin sat down in the sand and grabbed a toy car. "Well, well, indeed. Mother is pleased."

Chapter Thirty-Seven

IT WAS A TALKATIVE, HAPPY group that gathered around the dinner table. Keegan was freshly scrubbed. Instead of an electronic toy, he perched two of his action figures on the edge of the table. He was full of information about highway construction.

"I need a bulldozer," he said at last.

Kevin said to Megan, "Didn't you get him a bulldozer?"

"You were there," said Megan. "You might have mentioned it."

Kevin grinned. "Maybe for your birthday, Kee."

Karla came to the table in full face paint. She had tried some shadow effects, and her vampire face looked gaunt and haunting.

Krystal's eyes widened ever so slightly. "Karla, my dear, you look positively ghastly."

In vampire voice, Karla said, "Thank you, mother. The One Called Megan gave me a very useful book. Lots of good tips."

Krystal fluffed her napkin over her lap and murmured, "Lovely."

Cookie came in with a delicious smelling stew. She set the pot on the table, then stood waiting behind Megan's chair. Finally, she cleared her throat, loudly.

Karla looked up.

Cookie turned her hands over and asked, "Well?"

Karla raked the air with her black fingernails and hissed.

Cookie said, "That's more like it. Hold on, everyone, I made rolls to go with the stew."

Kevin said to Karla, "Distracted?"

Karla used her normal voice to answer. "I'm just thinking about the next chapter and how to add more color to my face. Don't you think bruising would be cool?"

Krystal lifted her wine glass. "Will you wear bruises to the wedding?"

Megan said softly, "I thought it would be wise to clear it with your mom."

Karla said, "Not at the wedding. That would be a bad omen. I'll save the bruises for a different occasion."

"You can make me decomposition green for the wedding photos," said Kevin.

"Cool!"

"Dreadful!"

"Sick!" But Keegan was grinning. "Can I be a vampire, too? For the wedding pictures?"

Karla sniffed the air. In vampire voice, she teased, "Did someone forget his garlic?"

Keegan pulled it out of his pocket and rubbed it on his head. "Safe now."

Cookie returned with a basketful of warm rolls.

"They smell heavenly," said Megan.

Cookie beamed as she returned to the kitchen.

Krystal dabbed at her lips with her napkin.

"Karla, Megan tells me your ability to apply theatrical makeup is quite an unusual talent."

Karla froze.

Megan could practically see the girl's wheels turning. It was clear that Krystal had never before considered her daughter's behavior in the light of creative expression.

At last Karla mumbled, "Thanks."

It was equally clear that the next few words stretched Krystal's maternal instincts to the max.

"If we're going to get creative with wedding photos, I would very much like to resemble Morticia Addams."

Karla's eyes flew open in disbelief. "Are you kidding me?" Her vampire voice dissolved into a teenage squeal.

"I'm quite serious," said Krystal. "I always enjoyed that program, and the cartoon series before that, and Morticia was an excellent mother and role model."

"Oh, my God! That would be totally awesome! Do I have a budget?"

Krystal allowed herself a small smile. "You may consider yourself funded."

Chapter Thirty-Eight

MEGAN AND KEVIN EXCHANGED glances of shared appreciation during the rest of the meal as Karla bubbled over with ideas. It had taken Kevin half an hour to convince his mother that trying a different tactic with Karla might produce different results.

By the end of dinner, it was also clear that Krystal's seamstress would require reinforcements. But Krystal didn't seem to mind.

After dinner, Kevin took Megan for a stroll through the stables.

Megan smiled to herself when he took her hand. His broad shoulders and handsome features seemed completely at home on the ranch.

Kevin stopped by a stall where a pale palomino nickered a greeting.

"Hello, Honeybun. Yes, I have some sugar cubes for you." He held his hand out flat and Honeybun nuzzled his palm. The sugar cubes were gone.

"Here," said Kevin, pulling Megan's hand up. "Make friends." He set two sugar cubes on Megan's palm.

Honeybun's lips tickled Megan's fingers as she accepted the sugar.

"Her lips are so soft," marveled Megan.

"I take it you haven't had much experience around horses."

"None. I used to pray for one when I was a little girl. The closest I got was a toy barn and some plastic animals for Christmas one year." She stroked Honeybun's nose.

"You'll have time to learn as much as you want here."

Megan cupped Honeybun's chin in her palm. "Kevin, your mother said that after the wedding I would be the lady of the house. Does that mean you plan an extended stay here on the ranch?"

"It's necessary," he said. "Once I inherit, I'll have to get much more involved in the running of the place. Zach has kept me posted over the years, even when I didn't want him to. I think Zach was the only one who ever really expected me to fulfill the terms of the trust."

"But your mother arranged a wedding for you!"

"For us," said Kevin softly. "You know, a week ago I didn't think I could do it. I thought we were going to lose it all to my father's moneymaking schemes and Wall Street wagers. I'd been looking for someone who could basically just stand next to me and say, 'I do.' And then you walked into the office." He paused to move a lock of her hair behind her ear. "You were a vision, with your angelic beauty. You practically glowed."

Megan blushed at the compliment. "I probably did glow," she said. "Six months in the hospital leaves a girl rather pale."

Kevin's smile loosed an internal flock of butterflies.

"I'm just saying," he continued, "when I placed that ad in the paper, I never expected I would actually find someone I could love."

Megan's heart pounded and her lips parted.

"Love?" she whispered.

Kevin leaned in and kissed her warmly.

Megan melted against him, letting the kiss take over. A tiny voice in the distance of her mind was asking how his lips could be so soft and warm and still deliver an electric charge? Should she ask Kevin about that? Maybe later. Next week would be soon enough. Could she stay here in the stable, kissing Kevin, for seven days? Easy. Maybe even forever.

Honeybun had different ideas. She pushed Kevin with her head and he had to step backward to keep his balance.

A moment later Zach's voice floated on the evening air.

"I'll just check the tack room."

Megan giggled. "Honeybun was telling you someone was coming."

Zach entered the stable.

Kevin wiped a hand across his mouth and scuffed at the hay-covered floor.

"You two lovebirds looking for some privacy? Or are you hiding out from your father?"

Chapter Thirty-Nine

KEVIN'S JAW TENSED and his hands balled into fists. "I thought he was staying at the hotel with his legal team."

"Evidently not," said Zach. "Just thought I'd give you a heads up." He nodded at Megan. "Ma'am."

Kevin turned to Megan. "I'd better go inside and see what's going on. You can wait out here if you like. Dad never sets foot in the stables. That's probably why I used to spend so much time out here."

"No," said Megan. "I ran from him once because he caught me off guard. I won't let that happen again. I'll go with you."

Kevin straightened his shoulders, feeling once again that Megan was more than worthy of his affection.

Together, they entered the house through the kitchen. They could hear Douglas Wake in the dining room, raging at Karla.

"I've had it with this vampire crap! You're going to school in Switzerland. I've already reserved a spot for you."

Krystal stood clutching the back of a dining room chair.

"Douglas, let's discuss this privately."

"I'm through with private discussions," he roared. His green eyes glinted cold and hard in the light from the chandelier. "I'm stating out loud and with witnesses," he stressed as Kevin and Megan entered the room, "that I am fed up with this costumed nonsense! Last month she told the wife of one of my managers that the low-necked dress she was wearing attracted vampires like corpses attract maggots! You heard her. You were there!"

Krystal's voice of reason countered with, "That woman barely had a dress on at all."

"That's not the point! The school officials told me we can deliver Karla any time because they offer a year-round curriculum. So I'm putting you on notice, young lady." He shook his finger at Karla. "Once this ranch transfers to my control next week, you are headed for Switzerland!"

Karla's reaction startled Kevin. She transformed herself from a quiet meek costumed child into a shrieking hellcat. She held her fingers like claws and slashed them through the air as her father approached. She alternated between shrieking and hissing, and she half-crouched as she bounded around the perimeter of the table, avoiding his grasp.

"You insufferable little brat! Your mother got you out of that hospital way too soon." He turned long enough to snap at Krystal, "You think I believed that cockamamy story about them not wanting to keep her? I know what you did!" Back to Karla, "Hold still!" He grabbed for her.

Karla eluded him by scuttling under the dining table, surrounding herself with chairs. She huddled there, hissing and clawing whenever her father made a move.

Kevin had had enough. He stepped into his father's space, forcing Douglas to back up a foot.

"Enough! Stop this nonsense now." His voice was deep and firm, and it carried the implicit promise that if Douglas did not stop, Kevin would make him regret it.

Douglas Wake puffed up and glared at his oldest son.

"You've got some nerve showing up to meddle in family affairs after all these years. You abandoned her!" He pointed at Karla. "And you abandoned your mother! But here you come running back when you smell money."

Kevin drew himself up his full height. In that moment, he realized that he was now taller than his father, and his summers as a lumberjack had added forty pounds of muscle to his frame. In measured tones, his anger barely under control, he spoke.

"I did not abandon anyone. You chased me away at eighteen. But at least I was ready for college. Now you're trying to send Karla away before she's old enough to fight back! You will never control this ranch, and you won't send my sister away for being different, either."

Douglas had to bend his head back to look Kevin in the eye. That fact was not lost on him. Nor was the very real presence of Kevin's physical bulk. His complexion darkened, but he said nothing.

Karla took advantage of the lull to scramble out from under the table and run for her room.

Kevin finished with, "I used to think you were a big man. Now I realize that you're just a bully." He held out a hand to Megan. "Let's go talk to Karla."

Chapter Forty

KEVIN KNOCKED SOFTLY ON KARLA'S DOOR.

"Go away!"

"Karla, you're not going to Switzerland."

A few seconds later, the door opened. The shades were drawn. The room was dark except for the illuminated skull that Megan had given her.

"Come in."

Kevin and Megan entered.

"May I turn on a lamp?" asked Kevin. "I'd like to see your face."

Karla turned on her bedside lamp. The room was cluttered with the treasures of its teen occupant. A laptop sat open on an antique desk. The chest of drawers was draped with clothing, as were the chair and the bed. The book on makeup was open on the bed as well. Two spaces were organized and tidy. One was the dressing table where jars and tubes of theatrical makeup awaited Karla's attention. The other was the art table near the window. The Victorian wallpaper was barely visible behind the sketches Karla had tacked to the walls.

Megan was drawn to the art right away. "These faces are amazing."

"Thanks," said Karla. "Mom and dad think they're the product of a sick mind."

Kevin said, "All your clothes are black."

Karla's brows drew together. "Not exactly." She pointed out different items. "Onyx, charcoal, thunderhead. Shall I go on?"

Kevin gave his sister a hug. "No need. I see what you mean. You know, I think mom is starting to come around. She wants to be part of the photo extravaganza. That's great, right?"

Karla nodded. "But it won't matter if dad is here. He'll forbid it, and Krystal will cave."

Without thinking Megan said, "Survival mechanism."

"What?" Karla looked puzzled.

Megan perched on the foot of the bed. Kevin joined her. Karla straddled her desk chair.

Megan explained. "Krystal lives with an overpowering man with anger issues. Sorry, Kevin, but that's so obvious to the outsider. Even you see it now. You called him a bully."

"He is," said Kevin. "I had to be away from it for six years before I could recognize it."

"And Krystal has developed behaviors to calm him down. She's always controlling her voice, governing her words, and trying to ameliorate the situation. Those behaviors are her survival mechanism."

Karla tilted her head to one side. "So that's why she never fights back? That drives me crazy. Once I told her she doesn't love me because she doesn't defend me when dad goes ballistic. I didn't realize she was trying to calm him down."

Megan turned a hand over. "That's because your survival mechanism is so different," she said. "You keep your father at bay by becoming a vampire and scaring the crap out of him. Did you see his face when you started shrieking?"

Karla smiled behind a hand. "That's not easy, you know? I had to practice those moves."

Kevin nodded. "I believe it. You scared the heck out of me, too."

"So, how can you be sure dad won't send me to Switzerland?"

"Because your mother won't let him," said Kevin. "And I'll back her up. Dad's a lot worse than I remember him, and he was bad when I was eighteen. I think his behavior is affecting his work. Maybe that's why he's counting on getting control of the ranch and the money in the Fineman trust. I also think he's had someone spying on me."

"Someone named Wong," said Karla. "I heard him talking on the phone one day."

Kevin deflated. "Oh, no! Not Jeffrey!"

Megan touched his leg. "I'm so sorry."

"I thought Jeff was my best friend."

Megan pulled her head back. "Your chauffeur is your best friend?"

Kevin rolled his eyes. "Okay, I knew I couldn't fool you forever. Until I take over the trust, I am not a wealthy man. My mother has been sending me an allowance every month for school. I got my degree in record time, but she kept sending money. And then I found out she told dad I was in graduate school so she could keep sending me cash. I let it build up in a bank account, and I stashed a bunch in my safe deposit box. I was using it to convince women I was super rich, because I thought that would be the only way to convince someone to marry me so I could inherit the trust. And part of that was hiring my best friend— my so-called best friend, the traitor—to play my chauffeur and drive the rented limo."

"Oh." It was a thoughtful syllable, full of concern and realization.

"Thanks to you, I *will* get control of the trust, and your medical bills will be paid. You don't have to worry about that. We have a prenup, remember?"

"Oh, that. I'm not worried. After meeting your family and knowing you're giving up your freedom so they can be assured of their own inheritance, I knew you were a man of your word." She reached out and squeezed his hand.

Karla's eyes were big as plates. "You mean, you guys are playing parts? You're just acting?"

"No!"

"No!"

Kevin looked at Megan, and Megan met his gaze.

"No, we're not acting," said Kevin. "I love Megan very much."

Megan's eyes grew bright. "And I love Kevin."

Karla looked relieved. "Then the wedding is still on?"

"Definitely," said Kevin.

"Too late to get out of it now," teased Megan.

"Good. Because if I end up in Switzerland, I'm going to run away from that school and come back and bite your necks."

There was a knock at the door. Kevin went to open it.

"Come in, mom."

"You can leave the door open," she said. "I convinced Douglas that he should stay in town with his legal team. I reminded him that his blood pressure suffers every time he flies into a rage, and it would be a shame if he were to have a stroke before the lawyers made a determination."

Megan's brow furrowed. "But I thought if Kevin was married before his twenty-fifth birthday, the result was cut and dried."

"Technically, yes," said Krystal. "But never underestimate a stubborn man with a corral full of lawyers. I'm sure he'll contest. But hopefully he won't have a leg to stand on."

Kevin, Megan, and Karla stared at the floor.

Megan broke the silence. "Where's Keegan?"

Krystal's expression softened. "He's out in the horseshoe pit playing with his new toys. It turns out Garcia has two little boys nearly Keegan's age. The three of them are building a city of roads in the sand. Zach gave them some small packing boxes from the office. Now they're making garages. I have to bring him in soon. The light is fading."

Megan stood up. "Speaking of Zach, I need to talk to him about something."

Kevin stood as well. "And mom, could I have a word?" He ruffled Karla's hair. "Yuck. Your hair is hard!"

"It's called hairspray, brother. I'm fourteen, remember?"

Kevin smiled at her, and followed his mother out of the room.

Megan hurried off to find Zach.

Kevin pulled his mother aside at the end of the corridor. "I just wanted to suggest that you be careful when dad and Zach are both around."

Krystal looked puzzled. "I am always careful when your father's around. But Zach would never hurt me."

Kevin rubbed his hands on his jeans. "Megan saw you and Zach together on the porch yesterday. Five minutes you were out there. When you left, she said it was obvious you were in love."

Krystal looked impressed. "She's very astute."

"Mom? You mean she's right?! Aren't you worried about dad's reaction?"

"Oh, Kevin. You're still so young in so many ways. Your father knew I was in love with Zach from the very beginning."

Chapter Forty-One

Thursday, June 28

The morning dawned bright and fresh. The heat wouldn't conquer the day until ten or later. Megan bounced downstairs to the kitchen. Just as she'd hoped, Keegan was spreading peanut butter on a thick slice of toasted homemade bread.

Cookie smiled at Megan and poured her a cup of coffee.

"Good morning, Keegan," said Megan, as if she could care less that he was at the table with her.

"Hi." Keegan held his toast in one hand and punched at the screen of his iPad game with the other. It was propped against his new toy dump truck.

Megan gave him points for combining his two favorite pastimes.

"You got peanut butter on your screen."

"Wipes off," said Keegan.

Megan spread butter on a slice of toast. "You need help cleaning your fingers. I have just the thing."

Keegan shot her a glance. "You're crazy." Then remembering the gifts she'd given him, he added, "Super nice, but crazy."

"I know. But aren't you curious?"

"Nope." He shoved toast in his mouth. Now he had peanut butter on both cheeks.

"That's perfect! Whatever you do, don't wipe that off."

Keegan pulled his face away from the iPad and gawked at her. "Does Krystal know you're telling me not to wipe my face?"

Megan leaned in close and whispered, "I have a secret weapon. Want to see?"

Keegan nodded.

"You have to finish your breakfast first. But try to get more peanut butter on your fingers, okay?"

Keegan turned to Cookie, his little face a question mark.

Cookie turned her hands over, as if to say, 'I don't have a clue.' She brought him a glass of milk.

Keegan lifted it with both hands. Now there were peanut butter smears on the glass.

Megan sipped her coffee, trying not to laugh. She had his attention.

Keegan crammed another big bite into his mouth and tried to talk around it.

Megan put a hand to her ear. "Did you hear something? Sounds like a transmission from outer space. Cookie? Did you hear it?"

Cookie drawled, "Sounds like Martians to me, too."

Keegan washed his toast down with more milk. Then he enunciated, "I said, this better be good."

"Good?" said Megan. "Just good? Oh, no, Keegan Wake—sorry, Keegan Fineman Wake—this is way better than good."

"I'm ready." Keegan reached for the dish towel Cookie had given him to wipe his face and hands on.

"Don't wipe," Megan reminded him. "We can't use the secret weapon if you wipe off all the peanut butter."

"Oh, right." He glanced over his shoulder to make sure Cookie wasn't looking. Then he plunged a finger in the peanut butter jar and smeared a glob across his chin. "I'm ready."

Megan couldn't help but laugh. She quickly cleared her throat and tried to sound serious. "All right, then. Let's go."

She led the way out of the kitchen through the back door. Keegan followed.

Megan marched across the grassy yard that surrounded the house, past the sandy horseshoe pit where Keegan's new toys lay scattered, and through the chain link gate. Keegan followed.

Megan headed for the large workshop where the business offices were located.

Keegan frowned. "Krystal told me never to go in there. She said those people are busy running the ranch."

"That's true, but I think it's okay if you have an escort."

"What's an escort?"

"You know, a grownup going in with you."

"Oh. Got it."

Megan entered the building and held the door for Keegan so he wouldn't have to touch it with his peanut butter fingers.

Keegan seemed surprised that he recognized the people they passed. "Hey, that's Garcia! Hi, Mister Garcia! Hi, Zach. You have your own room in here?"

Zach grinned at Keegan. "This is my office."

"Dad's office is in a skyscraper. And it doesn't have cement floors."

Zach rubbed his chin. "Hmmm. Well, we don't have many skyscrapers around here. This will have to do, I guess. Where you headed?"

Megan tipped her head to one side. "I told Keegan I had a secret weapon for cleaning peanut butter off his face and hands."

Zach's eyes twinkled. "Oh, yeah. Clear to the end and to the right."

"Thanks. Come on, Keegan."

"Does Zach know about this machine?"

"I never said it was a machine," said Megan innocently. "Here we are. Come on in."

She stepped into a cool, quiet room. Instead of furniture, there was a long piece of plywood stretching from wall to wall, separating the back of the room from the door. A large yellow Lab reclined on a dog bed in the corner with two healthy pups frolicking around her.

"That's Buttercup!" Keegan's eyes grew large. "Buttercup had puppies!" He clambered over the low wall and fell to his knees. One black pup and one yellow pup leaped up to lick the peanut butter off his chin.

Keegan giggled with delight. "Look! They're cleaning my fingers, too!"

"I told you I had a secret weapon. Aren't they cool?"

"They're kind of big for babies," said Keegan, between giggles.

"Labs are big dogs. They're three months old. Just right for leaving their mother."

Keegan looked horrified. "Where are they going?"

"Not far," said Megan. "Just from here to the main house."

"Really? They're going to live in the main house?"

"Sure. My dog is going to sleep in my room and watch TV with me and eat in the kitchen."

"Oh." Keegan drooped. "You get one of the puppies?"

"Yes, I do," said Megan. She joined him inside the enclosure and lowered herself carefully to the sawdust that covered the dirt floor. The puppies alternated between Keegan and Megan, leaping and grabbing at hands and clothing.

"What's going to happen to the other puppy?" asked Keegan, bleakly.

"Well, that depends on you."

"Me?!"

"Yes. Do you think you can spare the time from your iPad to take care of a puppy?"

Keegan squealed with delight. The puppies began to bark. "Yes! Yes! I get a puppy! I get a puppy!"

Megan laughed. "What are we going to name them?"

Keegan held up his partially cleaned hands. "Peanut Butter!"

"You can't name them both Peanut Butter."

Keegan pulled the black pup into an embrace. "Chunky!" he cried. "Mine is named Chunky Peanut Butter."

Megan smiled and cuddled the yellow pup. "And mine is named Creamy. How's that?"

Keegan's eyes were bright with tears of joy. "That's perfect," he said, burying his face in Chunky's black fur.

"I agree," said Megan, planting a kiss on Creamy's muzzle. "Absolutely perfect."

Chapter Forty-Two

HALF AN HOUR LATER, both pups were frolicking with Keegan on the fenced lawn. Buttercup followed them to the grass and promptly fell asleep under a tree. Zach stood grinning at the sight, thumbs hooked in his belt.

"They'll need collars and leashes," said Megan. "Do you think I can get a ride into town?"

Zach pulled out a ring of keys. "Take my truck."

"The one Kevin learned to drive in? I'm sure I couldn't handle that one."

Zach laughed. "No, that's an old ranch truck. Mine is over yonder, the blue Ford."

Megan's innards soured with fear, but she took a deep breath and accepted the keys. "Thanks. I'll be careful."

Megan stepped into the house to let Cookie know where she was headed. "I'm not sure where Kevin is. If he asks, let him know, okay?"

"Will do. He's in a meeting with his mother, by the way. The Fineman legal team has arrived." Cookie rolled her eyes.

"Good grief," said Megan. "Do you and Zach have legal teams, too?"

"Nope. We're just plain old working folk."

Megan smiled. "Just like me! I'll be back soon." She headed for Zach's truck.

Before she drove fifteen feet, Karla came running out of the house. "Wait! Wait!"

Megan stopped. "Hi, Karla. What's up?"

"Take me with you, please! I want to get some magazines."

"Sure. Get in."

Karla climbed into the cab. Her long nails were still painted black, and her clothes were onyx and charcoal, but her face was scrubbed clean. She pulled a small white lens container out of her pocket and popped her yellow lenses out of her eyes. She turned a smiling face to Megan.

"You have the same hazel eyes as your brother! I knew you would," said Megan. "Hey, where do you get those yellow ones, anyway? I saw them for sale once in San Francisco, but nowhere else. What's your secret?"

"Promise not to tell?"

"Cross my heart." Megan pulled out onto the two-lane highway.

"A few months ago my parents were freaking out because they kept searching my room and couldn't find my supply. And they couldn't figure out how I was getting them or anything."

"I heard about that," said Megan.

"I send money to one of my friends at school through PayPal. She buys the lenses and ships them to me in a big bottle of vitamin C. They moved that vitamin bottle a dozen times when they searched my room, but they never once opened it to look inside."

Megan laughed. "That is so clever! Hey, are they one-size-fits-all?"

"Yes."

"Do you think I could wear a pair for the photo session?"

Karla squealed with delight. "That would be totally awesome!"

Megan grinned. The ride into town was so full of conversation, she didn't have time to be nervous, not even when a large cattle truck barreled down the highway in the opposite direction.

Eagle's Toe was small enough to have slanted parking spaces along the main street but big enough to have a selection of shops and a couple of nice hotels to appeal to the tourists looking for antiques or a quiet meal or a few days of peace and quiet. Megan pulled into a parking spot in front of a bookstore.

"I'll be in here," said Karla. "The Feed and Grain Store makes me sneeze. It's just up this street two blocks and one block over."

"I'll walk it," said Megan. "I'll meet you back here in thirty minutes. Can you entertain yourself for that long?"

"In a bookstore? Give me a break. I could live in there."

Megan grinned. "Save a few for me."

The Feed and Grain Store had everything a rancher might need, including a splendid selection of leashes and collars. Megan pulled out the measuring tape she'd marked with the puppies' neck size and began double-checking collar lengths against it. She chose four, two rolled leather collars and two martingales for better control during walks. They looked puppy friendly and the salesperson showed her how the collars wouldn't tighten on their necks. The chain portion merely pulled the cloth collar closed so the puppy couldn't squirm out of it in a dangerous or exciting situation. She also picked out two leashes.

As the cashier rang up her purchases, a Cadillac pulled into a parking space in front. The sun gleaming off the car's grille sent patterns of light skittering across the wall, like a little devil dancing a jig.

Megan took her plastic bag and headed for the door.

Blocking her path was Douglas Wake.

Megan pulled herself inward, but stood her ground. "Excuse me," she said coldly. "I'm leaving."

Wake hesitated, then stepped aside and waved her through. "May I have a word?"

Megan kept walking. Wake strode beside her.

"I realize you saw me at my worst out at the house," he said, calmly. "I apologize. My rude manners had nothing to do with you, and yet I took out my frustrations by yelling. Sometimes its a curse, being a man. I was born with a big voice, and it gets out of control."

Megan wasn't sure what to make of Wake's change in attitude. She offered a noncommittal, "Okay," and kept walking.

"May we sit for a moment and chat? I realize that after Friday, you will be my daughter-in-law, and I don't want you thinking your father-in-law is a monster."

Megan wavered. He seemed sincere. Maybe he was really extending an olive branch. After all, even though he didn't know it yet, they were already related by marriage.

Or did he know?

No better time to find out. Megan stopped abruptly and sat down on a quaint bench outside an ice cream shop.

Wake looked pleased. "Can I buy you a cone?"

"No, thank you. I'm on a schedule. Please say what you have to say and I'll be going."

Wake sat at the other end of the bench.

They were still too close for Megan's comfort, but she reminded herself that they were in public, and after all, this was not her fly-off-the-handle father who used to embarrass her publicly. Wake was a businessman and should know how to control his public image.

"I just wanted to let you know," he began, like a father offering a daughter advice, "that Kevin is a fine young man. He'll make a wonderful husband."

"That's good to hear." Megan let her guard down a bit.

"And if I had picked a bride for him myself, she couldn't be any prettier than you."

Megan looked away and rolled her eyes, but she leaned back on the bench and said, "Thanks."

"I do want you to come into this marriage with your eyes open," he continued, with oily assurance. "And that's why it's important for you to know that Kevin doesn't have a dime in his own name. I know he promised to pay off your medical bills—"

Megan shot up off the bench. "How did you—?"

"Now, now, I'm a businessman." He continued in the same calm vein. "Surely, Kevin told you I have my spies."

Megan's heart was pounding, but she forced herself to sit back down on the edge of the bench. "Was that your man in Tahoe with the binoculars?"

"Yes. Not a very adept employee, but he has his uses."

Megan's eyes darted back and forth. "How did he find us?"

"Well, tracing the credit card purchase of the airplane tickets was easy enough. My spy in Seattle told me about the trip to Reno. My man there floundered a bit when you rented the car. Wasted valuable time trying to decide what to do. Finally called me and I told him to grease a few palms behind the rental car desk, and sure enough, those cars are equipped with GPS locating devices. For the right price, the clerk told him you were at Lake Tahoe. Gave him the exact location."

The man's calm demeanor was even more maddening than his rage of the night before.

"I know about your prenup. I know about Kevin's search for a bride and his clever but misguided attempt to get around the requirements of the trust. And frankly, I admire him for that. He's more like me than I ever suspected. He's got a true sense for business. Devious, like his old man. A chip off the old block. I couldn't be happier. Too bad it won't work. You see, it's not a marriage based on love. It's a last minute maneuver to acquire control of his mother's family money. And it won't work. I have my legal team all over it. So I just thought you should be aware, from the start, that you're marrying a fine young man, a man clever enough to take you in and make you think he really cares about you."

"He *does* really care about me!"

Wake chuckled darkly. "That's the best part. He fooled you just like I fooled his mother and his grandfather. Well, mostly his grandfather. That old coot wanted Krystal to marry a man with ambition, a man of business. It wasn't too hard to convince an impressionable young girl that I was madly in love with her. She was a lot like you. And Kevin is as good an actor as I was. But your motivation was money, so it's important that you know that he's as poor as you are. With that in mind, you might want to be thinking about how you're going to start paying off those bills."

Megan's stomach churned. The man was like a cobra, using his tone to lull her while his words dripped with venom. She clutched her plastic bag until her knuckles turned white. She stood up to leave.

"Oh, before you go, one more thing." With that line, his voice changed, and the implied threat was delivered with a cruel modulation. "I've already reported you delinquent to colleagues at three different credit agencies. Called in a few favors, as it were. The phone calls and debt letters will start arriving soon."

"Get away from me!" Megan's tone and volume attracted the attention of a number of shoppers who stared as she ran off down the sidewalk.

She glanced back over her shoulder, to make sure Wake wasn't following her. He was just sitting there, smiling smugly.

Chapter Forty-Three

MEGAN RUSHED INTO THE BOOKSTORE.

Karla was easy to find, since she was the only customer dressed in black at the end of a very warm June.

"Are you ready to go?"

Karla looked concerned. "What's wrong? You look upset."

"It's nothing. I just need to get back to the ranch right away."

"Okay." Karla picked up her purchases.

Megan pulled out cash. "This is faster." She wasn't sure she ever wanted to use a credit card again, after hearing Douglas Wake's sneering explanation of how he used it against them.

Back in the truck, Megan forced herself to calm down. She had to drive back to the ranch and deliver Karla in one piece. Then she could decide what to do.

It wasn't just that Kevin was broke. Everyone she knew was broke, before she met Kevin's family.

It was the specter of credit agencies pursuing her for her medical bills. The thought of it made her sick to her stomach! She never wanted to look Douglas Wake in the face again. She wanted to leave as soon as possible. She had to get away from that evil man.

She was grateful that Karla was quiet on the drive home. She needed all her concentration to pay attention to traffic.

She wasn't sure how she would do it, but Zach had been helpful so far. Creamy would be okay with little Keegan. Kevin was a big boy, he would get over it.

It felt like a fist squeezed her heart.

Kevin.

Could she leave Kevin? How could she love him so much in so little time?

And Karla and Keegan? She loved them, too, and they were not part of the plan!

She had to get away and think. She couldn't bear the thought of ever seeing Douglas Wake again.

She wanted to run to her mother, but she didn't even know where her mother was.

Karla leaned forward in her seat and squinted at Megan as she sped down the long ranch driveway.

"Megan? Are you crying?"

"No!" She wiped impatiently at her face. "I'll never cry again. No one will ever make me cry again!"

She braked hard, parking the truck in Zach's space. Leaving Karla to her own devices, Megan pulled the keys from the ignition and went in search of Zach.

She found him in the stable.

"Thanks for loaning me your truck," she said tightly, handing him the keys.

Zach examined her through narrowed eyes. "You okay?"

Megan took a breath and let it out. "No. I have to leave. I need a ride to an airport. Or a bus station. It doesn't matter."

"Does Kevin know you're going?"

Megan's hand flew to her mouth. A moment later, she said, "I can't talk to him right now." She was afraid if she saw Kevin standing in front of her, she would lose her resolve. The idea of leaving him was breaking her heart. But she would have to suggest an annulment. If he was as poor as she was, staying with him meant they would both be slaves to those stupid medical bills!

For the first time, she wished she'd died in the crash.

"I have to get away from here," she said firmly.

Zach nodded. "I see. I don't suppose you want to tell me what happened in town? Did Karla do something?"

"No, of course not. Karla's wonderful and kooky." Her voice threatened to fail her. "I just have to leave."

"You need to think things over."

"Yes. Away from here. Far away."

Zach made an understanding sound. "Okay, then. I've got some fences to check, so let's take the ranch truck."

Chapter Forty-Four

THE PARLOR WAS IN DISARRAY. Megan's wedding gown stood finished in one corner. Genevieve the seamstress was giving orders to two assistants. One of them began transporting the dress upstairs to Megan's room. Two other dress dummies were draped in black. Three sewing machines were set up along one wall. Three bolts of cloth were stretched across a folding table.

Kevin and Krystal stood near the parlor door.

"I see," said Krystal into her phone. Her voice sounded stronger every day. "Thank you, Mr. Ratigan. I'll relay the news to Kevin." She hung up.

"All good, I hope?" said Kevin.

Krystal shook her head. But before she could speak, Karla ran in from the kitchen, breathless.

"There you are! I've been looking all over!"

"What's wrong?" asked Krystal. "Is Keegan okay?"

"Yeah, he's fine. Playing with his friends and the puppies." She gasped for breath. "But something's wrong with Megan. Something happened in town, but I don't know what. She wouldn't say. She didn't talk at all on the ride home. Something awful," she gasped. She took a moment to catch her breath, then added ominously, "She was crying."

"Where is she?" asked Kevin.

"I don't know. It took me half an hour to find you guys."

"Why didn't you call?"

Karla rolled her eyes and glared at the two of them.

"Oh, right," said Kevin. "Mom, I think you need to restore her phone privileges."

"I was going to buy her a new one next week."

"Cool," said Karla. "But Megan was not a happy camper when she came and got me in the bookstore."

Krystal drew a worried breath, then touched Kevin's arm. "Your father!"

Kevin's brow darkened. "Karla, did you see dad in town?"

"I didn't, no, but Megan went to the Feed and Grain while I looked at books."

Krystal's voice hardened. "He's staying at the Cattleman's Inn."

Kevin growled, "Across the street from the Feed and Grain! Damn that man. I've got to find Megan." He turned and strode through the house. "Mom, alert the staff."

An hour later there was still no sign of Megan.

Kevin, Krystal and Cookie gathered in the kitchen. Kevin wiped a hand over his mouth. "Where could she go?"

"I hear a vehicle," said Cookie. "Maybe that's her."

Kevin rushed out the back door.

A green Ford Expedition pulled up next to the chain link fence near the kitchen door. Jeffrey Wong got out, looking happy but road weary.

"Hi, Kevin! I made it!"

Kevin went through the gate and approached Jeffrey. "Have you seen Megan?"

Jeff frowned. "She's here with you."

"She *was* here with me, you traitor!" Kevin took a swing at Jeff.

Jeff dodged and weaved. "Hey! What the hell?! Back off, dude. What is going on?"

"You! You've been feeding information to my father for years! How could you do that? Now we think he's chased Megan away. We can't find her anywhere."

Jeff looked offended. "Hey! I have covered your tracks for years. I can't stand your old man. The one time we met, he called me names. Why would I ever help him?"

"My sister Karla heard him talking to a man on the phone. He was calling him Wong."

Jeff's features slid into disappointment. "Patrick!"

Kevin's jaw worked. "He's been helping me with legal stuff for weeks."

"And he's my cousin," said Jeff. "Anything I talked about during family gatherings, he would have access to. That jerk! I knew he was ruthless about his business, but I never thought he'd stoop this low."

"My dad must have offered him a lot of money," said Kevin. "That's how he usually works. Sorry I doubted you, Jeff."

"Oh, man! Me and my big mouth. Before I left Seattle, I told my mother about our change of plans."

"You're allowed to talk to your family. You had no way of knowing. It's not like we were keeping national security secrets. But Patrick drew up the prenup."

Krystal took Kevin's arm to secure her balance. "So he knows that you and Megan only met last week."

Kevin nodded grimly. "I have to find Megan. Who knows what he might have said to her?"

Cookie wiped her floured hands on her apron. "You come in and eat, young man. Did you drive all the way here from Seattle?"

"Yes, ma'am," said Jeff.

Krystal said, "Kevin, we'll take care of Jeff. You go find Megan."

Chapter Forty-Five

KEVIN STOOD FOR A MOMENT, considering his options. He realized he hadn't seen Zach around either. He trotted to the metal office building and stuck his head inside.

"Mrs. Garcia? Have you seen Zach?"

"No, sir. But he had fences to check, so he's probably working."

"Is your husband around?"

"No. Mr. Zach sent him on an errand to Denver."

Kevin felt a flash of panic. "Not in the last hour, I hope!"

"Oh, no. He told him yesterday that today he would go to Denver. My Checo, he left at nine this morning."

"Okay, thanks." At least Garcia wasn't driving Megan to the airport.

"Oh, Mr. Kevin, I think the ranch truck is back now," said Mrs. Garcia. "So maybe Zach is back, too."

Kevin stepped outside in time to see the ranch truck pull behind the stable. He trotted to the stable and came to a halt next to Honey's stall.

Honey snuffled and threw her head back, but when she saw Kevin, she reached out with her nose to be petted.

"Not now, Honeybun," said Kevin. "I'm in a hurry." But he couldn't disappoint her. "Okay. Just for a few moments." He laid one hand on her face and immediately felt calmer.

172

Zach's voice came from deeper in the stable. "I told you, didn't I? It's hard to rush when you're holding a brush. Or in this case, touching the horse's nose. You looking for someone?"

Kevin turned to face Zach. "How is it you always know what's happening in my life?"

"Maybe because I been there before you."

Kevin was rubbing Honey's chin now. "Where is she, Zach? Did she tell you where she was going?"

"Megan?"

Kevin gave Honey one last pat and stepped away. He was too agitated to leave his hands on her for long.

"We think my dad said something to her in town. He'd say anything to chase her away. I just found out he's had a spy in Seattle watching my every move. So he knows that Megan and I only met last week. But I love that girl. A man can fall in love in a week, can't he?"

"People fall in love at first glance," said Zach. "You could fall in love a thousand times in a whole week."

"Well, maybe I'm slow," said Kevin. "But I knew she was special when I first met her. And then, watching her with my family? She's perfect. Everything was going great. And then my father entered the picture."

"You knew he would. He's got a lot invested in taking over this ranch. He'll do whatever he has to do, get rid of anybody who stands in his way. Lord knows he's tried to get rid of me. But I'm a tougher nut to crack than young Megan."

"I need to find her before she does something foolish. I need to tell her how I feel."

"Even if it means losing your inheritance? The trust fund? The ranch?"

Kevin spread his hands. His voice betrayed his anguish. "What good does all this do me without her?! She made this place come alive for me. I saw an old-fashioned house. She sees a Victorian treasure. I saw my sister spiraling into mental illness. She sees a creative genius and finds a way to bring Karla out of her shell. Keegan was becoming more and more cut off from the world. Now he has friends! If Megan leaves, it all falls apart."

Zach squinted into the distance for several seconds. At last he turned to look at Kevin again, and his eyes were a bit brighter than before.

"She's over to Fineman's Pond, in the fishing cabin. She needed a safe place to hole up for a while and think."

"Thanks, Zach." Kevin turned to leave, but Zach caught his arm.

"When you were a boy, spending your summers here, you looked up to me."

"I still do, Zach. You know that."

"Well, listen up real good. If you want me to respect you the same way, don't you come back here without that woman. It don't matter what your father says or threatens to do. There's no fortune on the planet big enough to make up for losing her. You understand?"

Kevin nodded, then extended a hand. "I'll bring her home."

Chapter Forty-Six

KEVIN HEADED BACK TO THE HOUSE, but checked the Ford for keys before he went in. Jeff had left them in the ignition. Kevin got in and drove carefully toward the rutted path that led to Fineman's Pond.

As he drove, he wondered what his father had said to her. Had he used the information from Patrick to hammer a wedge between them? Had he told her he was not the wealthy man he'd pretended to be? Kevin had already admitted to that. That couldn't be the problem. What could his old man have said?

The scary thing was, Douglas Wake could have said anything, and it didn't matter to him if it was true or not. He was ruthless. That was one of the qualities that had sent Kevin running clear across the country at eighteen. But Kevin was no longer a boy. He was a grown man, and he had grown in every way. Physically, his father no longer frightened him. Kevin knew if he had to, he could defeat his father in a fight. Not that he would ever want to fight the man. But Megan did not have the reassurance of physical superiority. She was still recovering from her accident. She had financial worries. What could his father have used against her?

Whatever it was, Kevin would protect her. He couldn't bear the thought of losing her. It was just too painful. He could not return to life before Megan. Looking back to those days, it felt like he had no heart, no soul, no joy. He got up every day and wished he was someone else.

Since meeting her, he wanted to be himself, because that's who she had fallen in love with. He was sure she had. He could feel it.

Fifty feet from the cabin, he parked the Ford under the lean-to horse shelter he and Zach had built years before when they spent summers fishing at the pond. He pocketed the keys and headed quietly for the cabin.

He started to enter unannounced, but caught himself and knocked softly.

A moment later, Megan called, "Who is it?"

Kevin wanted to barge in but she hadn't said come in. He knocked again.

A few seconds passed, and after what felt like an hour, the door opened.

Megan's blue eyes were red-rimmed and her nose was pink. She made a little sound when she saw Kevin, and then she tried to close the door.

But he was fast. He blocked it with his boot.

"Megan, please let me in."

"Your father made everything extremely clear," she said. "I know I signed on to be your temporary bride, and it's not your fault I let myself fall for you. But I thought you fell for me, too! I thought you really cared about me. Now I know the truth. You were just proving to your father that you can be as mean and thoughtless as he is!"

"No, no! That's not the truth, I swear." Kevin stepped inside and pushed the cabin door shut behind him. "So, we guessed right. When Karla told us how upset you were, mother immediately thought my father had cornered you and said something to upset you." He stepped toward her, but she backed away.

"You told me up front that this was a job, a business deal," she said. "You would pay my medical bills, and in return I would help you fulfill the obligations of the family trust. I was an idiot to pretend it was more than that."

"No, Megan, I'm the idiot. I fell for you hard. I couldn't even sleep with you in Reno after we got married because I cared so much about you that I wanted you to love me before we actually touched each other. I wanted to make love to you, not have sex with you."

His words stopped her cold. "Do you mean that?" she whispered.

"Yes," he whispered back. He took another step forward. She was pressed against the wall of the cabin now and could retreat no further.

"What did he say to you?"

"He told me you were more like him than he ever suspected. He said you fooled me, just like he fooled your mother."

"That bastard!"

"And he, he, he," she stuttered, not sure about whether to share the rest.

"Go on," said Kevin gently.

"He said he has proof you're not fulfilling the requirements of the trust and he can prevent you from inheriting. He's reported my medical bills to a collection agency! And if you're as broke as I am, and I stay, then you'll be burdened with those bills, too! So I was thinking the best thing I could do for you is leave. Get an annulment."

"No!"

Kevin opened his arms, and Megan stepped into them.

"You can't leave me. And I won't let you have an annulment. I love you, Megan. My father was lying. He was playing on your worst fears. Patrick Wong has been spying for him, and he told him about the prenup. You've never been in debt, so you don't know how these things work. He was saying whatever it took to get you to run. I know enough about his business to know he can't just make a phone call and put you on a collection agency list. Only the hospital could do that. And thanks to you, come Monday, I will be a very wealthy man. Even if his lawyers take our lawyers to court, he doesn't have a leg to stand on. We were married in Reno!"

Megan leaned back to look in his eyes. "I don't think he knows that. His spy only caught up to us in Tahoe. He didn't know about our stop at the courthouse."

"Well, that's even better. He'll show up tomorrow at the wedding expecting to gloat and hold it over my mother."

"Does she know about Reno?"

"I've been trying to tell her. Even during our meeting with her legal team, those guys just keep talking. I still haven't had a chance to let her know."

He took gentle hold of Megan's arms. "Even if the worst happens, we stand a good chance in court. But it doesn't matter. Rich or poor, I have to have you in my life. Please say you'll stay."

"Oh, Kevin! I almost made a huge mistake!"

He kissed her forehead, then her cheeks, then her chin. "No, I'm the one who made the mistake. Megan, my old man can have it all. I don't care. I just want you."

"Oh, me, too!" She kissed him back, planting her lips across the bridge of his nose. Her breath was coming in quick little gasps, but she couldn't stop talking. "I want you, too! I don't care about the money. I'm a good waitress. I'll get a job and start paying my medical bills, a little every month. They'll just have to settle for that."

"I'll help you. I promised I'd pay them, and we're married. I'm your husband, and I'll find a way. You won't have to worry alone."

At last their lips found each other and speech was impossible. Megan surrendered to Kevin's arms. With one hand, Kevin reached out and closed the curtains over the cabin's single window.

Chapter Forty-Seven

Friday, June 29

MEGAN LAY BACK ON the sheets and sighed with pleasure.

"You all right?" Kevin lay beside her and traced one finger along her collar bone.

"I am so relaxed, I can hardly talk."

"What's that? You're mumbling," teased Kevin.

Megan grinned. "Call me Mrs. Wake."

"Yep, we're finally man and wife for real."

Megan thumped him gently with her hand. "I mean, literally. Say it out loud for me."

"Oh." Kevin tried to wipe the afterglow off long enough say formally, "Mrs. Wake."

"Now say, Announcing Mr. and Mrs. Kevin Fineman Wake."

He brushed his lips against her bare shoulder and murmured, "Announcing Mr. and Mrs. Kevin Fineman Wake."

Megan giggled.

"Now say, You're so hot I could die."

Kevin laughed.

"Hey, that's not funny," said Megan, forcing a pout. "Don't you think I'm hot?"

"Of course I do. I just think it's funny that your first official act as my wedded and bedded wife is to put words in my mouth like a ventriloquist."

"Not like a ventriloquist," objected Megan. "My lips are moving." She pushed her lips toward him and move them from side to side.

Kevin rolled onto his back and laughed again.

Megan smiled. "Laughing is good. Not very romantic, but good."

"Don't worry," said Kevin. "It will get romantic again very soon." This time when he laughed, it was a deep sexy rumble.

Megan giggled. "I'm just so relaxed. I don't think I've ever felt this mellow in my life." She sighed and threw one arm over her head. The sheets on the bed were very expensive, and that meant high thread count, and that meant slippery. Megan had no idea she was so close to the edge of the bed. The momentum of her arm started a slide that neither of them realized would take her off the edge until she landed, thump! on the cabin floor.

Kevin rushed to her aid. "Are you okay?"

Megan came up stark naked and laughing.

When it was clear she was okay, Kevin began laughing, too.

At last, Megan crawled back up on the bed. "What time is it? Heck, what *day* is it?"

They looked at each other and gasped.

"Our wedding day!" they chorused.

Kevin put a hand on her arm to keep her from bolting out of bed. "It's only a ceremony."

"I know, but your mother! Your little brother! He's wearing a suit for us, Kevin. That is huge."

Kevin looked miserable. "I was thinking more along the lines of my father."

Megan made a face. "I'm sure he'll think of some way to ruin the day."

"Well, he won't have that chance if we don't show up, and think how pissed he'll be about that." Mischief gleamed in Kevin's eyes.

"No way, Mister Wake. Missus Wake," she pointed at herself, "wants this wedding. I know it's your mother's party, and I didn't care one way or another when we first met. But now, there's Zach and Keegan and Karla, not to mention Cookie's buffet! I'm hungry."

"Okay, okay, I guess we're going to our wedding." Kevin sounded resigned.

Megan picked up a pillow and bopped him with it.

They were laughing again, but Megan cut the pillow fight off. "There will be time for that tonight. We have to go! Your mother will be frantic."

"And imagine the look on good old dad's face when we actually show up together." The anticipation goaded him into action. "Okay, let's go. Shower, clothes, and coffee. Then we'll head back. Hey, let me check the car. Maybe Jeff left some food in it." He grabbed his keys, pulled his boots on and scampered naked to the Ford.

Alone for a moment, Megan sighed and clasped a pillow to her bare bosom. She buried her face in it. It smelled like Kevin. It smelled like love.

A small twinge of regret threatened to mar the day. As a girl she daydreamed about sharing her wedding day with her mother. Six days ago she wasn't even sure she wanted to tell her mother what she was doing. Now she wished she'd wired that first thousand dollars to Guatemala with instructions and a map of Colorado. Of course, she'd had no idea then that Kevin would turn out to be the man of her dreams. The course of their romance was anything but ordinary. Even so, it hurt to know her mom wouldn't be there. But she would make it up to her somehow. And if her father even cared, she'd make it up to him, too.

Chapter Forty-Eight

AFTER A QUICK SHOWER, they dressed in a hurry, then took a decadent half hour to sip their coffee on the porch swing, watching the morning come alive. By eight o'clock they were on their way.

In half an hour, they were within sight of the house. Kevin spotted Zach emerging from the stable and gave a whistle.

Zach turned. When he spotted them, even from that distance they could see his smile. Zach lifted an arm in greeting, then headed back into the stable.

A few moments later, Keegan emerged, spotted them, and began to run toward them. On his heels were Chunky and Creamy, barking and frolicking.

"They're here! They're here!"

Megan slid out of the Ford and ran to greet Keegan and the pups. She hugged Keegan tight.

"I missed you, Megan" he said. "I was so afraid you were never coming back." His eyes teared up.

"Hey, hey, no tears today! It's my wedding day. We're going to have fun, okay?"

"Okay." He wiped his eyes and grinned. "Did you have breakfast?"

"No, and I'm starving!"

"Pancakes with peanut butter!"

Megan let him go and he ran for the big house.

Kevin slipped an arm around her. "You have the magic touch with Keegan." He kissed her temple. "I love that about you."

"I'd better go let your mother know I'm still here."

"Go on in. I'll join you soon. I'm starving."

Zach was leaning against the side of the stable. "You two look good together." He pulled his hat down a half inch in front, a cowboy's salute.

Megan rushed back for a moment, long enough to plant a kiss on Zach's cheek. "Remember our plan," she whispered.

Zach said, "Yes, ma'am."

She trotted off toward the house.

"What plan?" asked Kevin. "Are you keeping secrets with my wife?"

Zach winked at him. "I'm giving her away."

"Thanks, Zach." Kevin paused and stared down at his feet. "For everything."

"I'll see you up at the house. If you want breakfast, you'd better get a move on. It's going on nine o'clock."

Cookie was pouring batter on a big griddle. "Pancakes coming up. What about you, Kevin? You want pancakes? You're going to need your strength." Her rosy cheeks crinkled in a smile and she winked at him.

"Everyone seems to have something in their eyes today," said Kevin. He joined Keegan at the table where the boy was pushing toy cars along the red-checked tablecloth. The Labs were tussling in the corner. "Where's Megan?"

Keegan bounced back and forth in his chair. "She went to tell Krystal she's come back to walk down the plank."

"Down the aisle," Cookie corrected. "Walk down the aisle, Keegan."

Keegan shrugged.

Kevin said, "What do you think, Cookie? Should I go look for her?"

"I told her we'd give her ten minutes before we call the search and rescue team."

Chapter Forty-Nine

MEGAN KNOCKED SOFTLY on Krystal Wake's door. This wing of the house filled her with nostalgia for a past that was never hers. It was so lovely here, with old wooden floors and thick woven rugs, and white lace curtains blowing softly in the morning breeze from the window at the end of the hall. The walls were decorated with family photos and faded tintypes, stern faces in costumes from another century, but the long narrow table beneath the photos was festooned with fresh cut flowers from Cookie's garden. The effect was one of continuation and the passing on of a legacy. She didn't hear the door open. Krystal's soft voice startled her.

"You've come back."

"Oh! Yes, I wanted to let you know everything is fine. Kevin and I are going to have breakfast and then dress for the ceremony."

"Come in." Krystal stepped aside to let Megan enter.

The bedroom was bright and airy. The bed had already been made, and it was covered with a faded quilt. An overstuffed chair in the corner looked even more inviting with a book open face down on the arm. The window was flanked by book cases, and a window seat spanned the space between them. A large pine armoire stood against the opposite wall with a tidy row of suitcases stored beside it.

"Won't you sit?"

Megan perched on the window seat. "After I left so suddenly

yesterday, I thought I owed you an apology. I didn't go far. I just needed to think things over."

"I know. Zach told me."

Megan was mildly surprised. "Zach?"

Krystal smiled like the Mona Lisa. "He tells me everything," she said softly. "You went to the cabin. And later, he sent Kevin after you."

Megan's eyes grew wide. "Yes, that's right. And Kevin explained everything. And, well, we made up."

"I'm so glad." Krystal moved slowly to the overstuffed chair and sank into it. "I realize that most brides are more involved in planning their wedding day, but under the circumstances, I hope you don't mind too much."

"No, not at all."

Krystal made a questioning sound. "You mean, as long as you could make some changes."

Megan was puzzled for a moment, then understood. "Oh, you mean Karla."

"You know, we all have to learn how to behave at some point in life. I'm not sure you're doing her any favors." Krystal's criticism was tempered by her gentle tone.

"I know. But I'm an invader, joining the family on very short notice. I want Karla to remember this day as a time when she got to be herself, even if it makes for amusing wedding photos. I don't want her to resent my arrival as the day she had to put on a costume and parade around like someone's extra in a movie." Megan's memories colored her speech more than she realized.

"Sounds like you have a few resentments of your own," Krystal said softly.

"Don't we all?" Megan shook off the past of her own family and admired the bedroom. "This is a beautiful room, and a lovely house. How can you bear to leave it for New York?"

Krystal shrugged. "New York has its charms as well. But I am delighted that you admire the house so much." She caught her bottom lip with her teeth, choosing her words carefully. "I need to ask a question, and I'm not sure how to go about it." She sent her eyes right, then left, and whispered, "Walls can have ears in this high tech age we live in."

Megan nodded her understanding. "No need to worry, Mrs. Wake. I love Kevin very much, and I am so looking forward to sharing my life with him here in this very house. I hope we have your blessing, to continue on here at the ranch. If I had to leave it now, I don't know what I'd do. And someone has to care for Chunky when Keegan goes back to school."

"Now there is another matter," said Krystal, relaxing into her chair, "that we must discuss after the ceremony. Keegan is quite taken with you. And frankly, after seeing him outdoors in the sunshine, running and playing, instead of cooped up with his Wii and his iPad, I am quite taken with you myself."

Megan smiled. Those were the kindest words Krystal had spoken to her since she'd arrived. "He's a wonderful boy. He needs a playmate, and after growing up an only child, I am taking full advantage of the opportunity to be around him."

"So you really do enjoy having children around?"

Megan spread her hands. "Isn't it obvious?"

Krystal nodded. "Yes, more and more so. You are very much an open book, Megan. And I am so glad that Kevin has found someone to love. You know that his father is against this marriage?"

Megan made a face. "He made that very clear. That's what sent me running for the hills. But," she said, straightening her spine, "I'm not going to let some stuffed shirt candidate for Grinch of the Year scare me away from the man I love. My life has not been a bed of roses, you know. Kevin was a surprise. A wonderful, glorious surprise. I love him, and he loves me back, and I'm never letting go of that."

Krystal rested her head on the back of the chair and let a genuine smile lift ten years off her face. "Oh, Megan, my dear, I'm so thrilled to hear that! At last, the chain of fatherly curses has been lifted." She sat forward and levered herself up from the chair. She held her hand out to Megan who rose also. Krystal faced her and held both her young hands in perfectly manicured but somewhat chilly fingers as she spoke.

"When I was a young lady, I fell in love." Her gray eyes darkened toward wet stone. "And he loved me back. But we were from different worlds. My father was furious. He forbade it! He said if I married against his wishes, he would leave me penniless."

"But you married your love anyway," said Megan, thinking of Mr. Wake.

"No," said Krystal sadly. "I did not. I married Kevin's father instead. He was the man who had my father's seal of approval. Zach was my love. But I was weak. I gave in to my father's wishes. And I have paid for that decision every day since."

"Oh, I'm so sorry."

Krystal pulled herself together and managed another tiny smile. "You are very sweet. And you are stronger than I was. More importantly," she added, "Kevin is stronger than I was. Whatever happens, do not let *his* father ruin your lives together. I'm so happy for the two of you."

She pulled Megan's hands to her lips and planted a kiss on her knuckles.

"Welcome to the family, Megan."

Chapter Fifty

BY THE TIME MEGAN RETURNED to the kitchen, she barely had time for half a bagel before Cookie raised her hands in alarm and said, "Oh, my goodness, honey, you have to get dressed! It's ten o'clock! And you, too, Kevin. And what about Keegan? Who's helping you get dressed?"

"I'm a big boy. I can dress myself."

Kevin patted Keegan on the back. "These are special duds, brother. We both need help. I'll tell you what. You help me and I'll help you. Deal?"

"Deal."

"Grab your trucks. We better get moving." He tipped Megan's chin up and planted a warm kiss on her lips. "See you very soon, lovely lady."

Megan beamed. "My mouf is foo of bagow," she mumbled. "Sowwy."

Kevin laughed. "This is going to be fun." He kissed her again. "Go get dressed." He headed off with Keegan who had evidently allowed his trucks to transform into flying machines.

Megan swallowed. "I'll check on Karla!"

She took the other half bagel with her and headed for Karla's room.

"Knock, knock! Are you ready, Karla?"

"No! Go away!"

"Uh-oh," said Megan. She tried the knob. It was unlocked, so she entered carefully. "Karla? What's wrong? I thought we had this all planned."

Karla sat glumly on the edge of her unmade bed. Her suitcases were strewn about the room, unzipped and open. She was still in her black jammies. Her baby smooth feet looked incongruous with black toenail polish. Yesterday's mascara was rubbed across her cheeks.

Megan sat down next to her on the bed. "Hey, partner in crime. Where's your outfit? Your dog collar?"

"My father came by last night and said he'd kill me if I wore black to your wedding. So I'm not going."

Megan flashed fire. "Oh, for the love of—" She bit off the words she was about to launch in anger. She took a breath. "Listen to me, Karla. *I* want you at my wedding. I don't care what your father thinks. He's not getting married, I am! You are Kevin's only sister. It's time your father learned that other people have their own wants and desires." She covered her mouth. "You didn't hear that from me. But it's true. You hurry and get dressed. I want you in all your vampire glory. We are going to have awesome family wedding photos! Wear that cool dog collar, the one with tags, okay? And don't forget your wrist bling!"

Karla was almost afraid to believe her ears. "Really? You want me to wear my studs, too?"

"Totally! This is my party, right? I want all my important people there, looking and feeling like themselves! Now you get ready, because I have to go do my hair, my makeup and get my dress on in forty-nine minutes. Yikes!"

Just then, the sweetest voice Megan ever heard floated from the doorway. "Need some help, sweetie?"

"Mom? Mom! What!? How!? When!?"

Glenda Mully chuckled. "Oh, my little girl is getting married! You think I'd miss that?" She and Megan hugged until they had to break for air. "Oh, honey, don't cry!"

"But I'm so happy!"

Karla watched from her bed.

Megan turned. "Karla, this is my mother. Mom, this is Kevin's sister Karla. She's so cool! Wait until you see her all dressed for the wedding."

Karla's glum features broke into a grin. "I better shower fast," she said.

"Come on, mom, I'm so happy you're here. I really need your help, too." She chattered all the way to the bedroom where the wedding dress was draped over a seamstress's form. "How did you get here?" Megan stopped and glanced up and down the hall. "Did dad come?"

"Yes. He's downstairs, introducing himself around. You know your dad."

Megan nodded. "Never at a loss for words."

"Now come on," said Glenda. "We have work to do. I'll start your hair. You do your makeup. And we'll talk as we work. Now let's see. Where to begin. Okay, Monday dad and I got a phone call from a very nice Mr. Garcia who then put a man named Zach on the phone. And he told us you were getting married, and we were going to come as a special surprise. He gave your dad no chance to say no. I can't wait to meet that Zach fellow. He had your dad sputtering on the phone! And when he told us he was sending a private jet and we'd better get our keesters to Guate to meet the plane at La Aurora, you bet your father got moving! No one ever sent a private plane for us before."

"Guate?"

"That's what the locals call Guatemala City, the capital."

"When did you get to Colorado?"

"Yesterday afternoon. That nice Mr. Garcia was waiting for us when we landed, and he took us out to dinner and we stayed in a nice hotel, then up bright and early this morning to get here in time for the ceremony! Oh, your father grumbled, you know. And it's smack in the middle of the rainy season in Guatemala, and your father's old Jeep got mired in the mud on the way to the airport, because the only place that would have his mission is out in the boonies. You know, he thinks everyone needs him and he forgets that this is a modern nation with their own pride and their own churches. We mainly do volunteer work with orphans but it really gets your father's goat that he has to work under a local clergyman and can't take off on his own. And of course, he's not giving sermons, because his Spanish isn't good enough, and he's not ordained in that church."

"Enough, enough," said Megan, staying her mother's hand with the hairspray in it. "Mom, you're getting really excited. Let's save the missionary stories for after the wedding, okay? I want to hear it all, but I want to tell you about Kevin."

"Oh, of course you do! Silly me, I'm just so thrilled to see you, my little Meggers."

Megan stood and they embraced again. "Me, too, mama. This makes today officially the best day of my life. I'm so sorry I couldn't get hold of you to tell you I was out of the hospital."

"Thank God you're okay. That's the only way I was able to leave you. I had to go back when I did, because—well, that story can wait.

Let's just say, your father was in a pickle with the Guatemalan government. I couldn't let him go to jail."

Megan's eyes popped. "Okay, then," she said. "We will have some interesting stories to share at the reception."

"Are you expecting many guests, dear?"

"I have no idea. It was too short a notice for my college friends. And actually, you know, I wasn't that close to many people. I was working all the time."

"I know, dear." Glenda's face fell. "I'm so sorry we couldn't help you out."

"Don't be silly! You gave me five thousand dollars! And it made all the difference. You instilled in me a desire to stay debt free." She hesitated. "In fact, that's how I met Kevin." She changed the subject. "Here, help me get into this dress. It fit me day before yesterday. Let's just hope it still does. Ever since I left the hospital, I've wanted to taste everything."

"Hospital food can do that to you. Makes you want to eat everything that is *not* hospital food."

They laughed together.

The dress still fit. It zipped up easily.

"This is beautiful," said Glenda. "Very simple and elegant, and yet so extravagant."

"You mean the pearls and lace? Yes, I know. I absolutely adore it."

"Where ever did you find it? It looks like something you'd see in a New York bridal shop."

Megan cleared her throat. "Well, now, there's an interesting story behind the dress," she said, once again staring her marriage bargain in the face. How to explain in twenty minutes or less how she and Kevin met, then actually fell in love? And what if Krystal was right? What if the walls *did* have ears?

Then she clamped her mouth shut. She wouldn't put anything past Douglas Wake. She wouldn't chance giving him any ammunition, even if he seemed to know everything already. Besides, she didn't have time to explain it all to her mother at the moment.

Instead she said, "Kevin's mother Krystal gave me the gown as a gift. It was very sweet and thoughtful. Help me with my veil, mom."

"Oh, look, more lace and pearls! And these tiny artificial roses! Are those silk?"

"I think so, yes."

"My, my, my." Glenda looked wistful. "Do you want to know a secret?" She leaned close. "When your father and I had our church wedding, I couldn't afford a gown. I went to a costume shop and rented one! That's why I couldn't save it for your wedding day. Besides, it would have been two sizes two big. Because I was five months pregnant that day!"

"Mom! You never told me that!"

"Some things are better left unsaid, dear. I told you your father was a lot more persuasive in his youth? Well, he used quite a bit of that on me." Her eyes were round and held a you-know-what-I-mean look. "And after the blood test, I used quite a bit on him. I told him it wouldn't look good for a young pastor starting out to have an unwed mother haunting him every where he went."

"You didn't?!" Megan didn't know whether to laugh or be horrified. "You are amazing, mama."

"I did what I had to do, my dear. Just like always." She smiled with satisfaction, then changed the subject. "Where did you meet Kevin, dear?"

"In Seattle," said Megan, biting off her tendency to run on at the mouth with her mother and tell her everything. "He went to school there."

"Oh, I can't wait to meet him and learn all about his family!"

Megan smiled at herself in the mirror. *I'll try to stay one step ahead*, she thought.

Chapter Fifty-One

AT TEN TO ELEVEN, Krystal knocked on the dressing room door.

"Come in," called Megan.

Krystal's eyes lit up when she saw Megan in her dress.

"Mom, this is Kevin's mother, Krystal Fineman Wake. Krystal, this is my mom, Glenda."

"So happy to meet you," gushed Glenda. "Megan said her dress was a gift from you. What a wonderful thing to do for my little girl!"

Krystal maintained her reserve, but her gray eyes now held a glint of amusement. "She is the most deserving young woman I have ever met. She has made my Kevin a very happy man." Before Glenda could rush on, Krystal held up a hand. "Megan, dear, the minister is here. Your father is trying to talk him into sharing the ceremony."

Megan looked horrified. "Mom! Stop him, please!"

"I'm on my way," said Glenda, and she rushed out of the room.

Krystal smiled softly at Megan. "Your mother is lovely."

"Good, because my father is not."

Krystal laughed.

Megan had never heard her laugh before.

Krystal stepped forward and gave Megan an impulsive hug. "We seem to have more in common than I ever guessed," she said, returning to her reserved self. "Take a few moments to compose yourself, dear. We will not start without you." She turned to leave, then paused. "By the way, thank you for helping Karla. She just told her father she was dressing exactly as the bride requested. I wouldn't have missed that moment for anything." She left, closing the door silently behind her.

Megan stood in the quiet and examined her reflection in the mirror. Not bad for a last minute bride. Not bad for a well prepared bride. Not bad, period. Her mother had swooped her hair into a French twist and left a few tendrils loose to soften the effect.

She pulled the veil down over her face. Her heart skipped a beat. She looked like a fairytale bride. Time to go downstairs.

She left the room and walked to the end of the hall. She could hear voices below, and she could hear someone playing the organ. The sound of the Wurlitzer took her back many years to Sundays before her father's sermons when her mother would entertain the congregation with renditions of popular hymns. She listened more carefully, then smiled. It was her mother playing now, she would bet money on it! She heard her flub the same key change in "Blessed Assurance" that she had been flubbing since Megan was a child.

She headed down the stairs.

Zachary waited for her on the landing.

And so did her father.

Megan stopped cold.

Zach said softly, "We came to an agreement. One of us on each arm."

Vernon Mully did not look pleased, but he never looked pleased, so Megan nodded. "That's perfect."

She continued down the stairs with her escort. At the foot of the stairs, they stopped.

The double doors to the parlor were open and the room was full of people. Some of them were familiar, but at least twenty were unknown to her. She guessed that the dozen or so children were the offspring of the ranch employees. But the six men in dark blue suits were a mystery. Three of them were huddled in a corner with Kevin. She was pleased to see Jeffrey Wong at Kevin's elbow. The other three suits stood soldier-like behind Douglas Wake. None of them looked happy or comfortable.

Megan had no time to determine what was transpiring. Her mother glanced around when the first ooohs and aaaahs rose from the gathering. Everyone was admiring her dress, and she couldn't blame them. As soon as Glenda Mully saw her daughter standing between her escorts, she began playing the Wedding March. A murmur of anticipation swept through the ladies in the room. Those who were standing quickly took their chairs. When they did so, a lovely tapestry was revealed. It wasn't a red carpet, but the embroidered flowers, hearts and birds in flight depicted there provided an idyllic runway for the bride.

Kevin shoved papers at the blue suits in his corner, and strode to the front of the room where the minister awaited him. Once there, he turned and caught Megan's eye, and they shared a private smile. Then he gave her a tiny nod of encouragement.

Megan Mully Wake began her walk down the aisle.

Chapter Fifty-Two

"HOLD IT! HOLD EVERYTHING!" Douglas Wake, flanked by his lawyers, raised an open hand to halt the proceedings.

Krystal's gray eyes flashed fire. "Sit down, Douglas! This day belongs to Kevin and Megan."

Douglas turned and glared at her. "You and I both know this is about a lot more than a wedding party. I have information that will affect everything that happens here, and everything that happens afterward."

Krystal raised herself carefully from her chair. "You are such a drama queen," she snapped. "Let these young people have their wedding!"

Douglas held up three pages of legal-sized paper. "This wedding is a farce! I have evidence here that proves it!"

Megan's insides ached with tension.

Kevin spread his hands. "Dad, for the love of God, you don't know what you're talking about."

"I'm talking about this prenuptial agreement my people uncovered."

Kevin bristled. "You mean, your spies. I know all about them. Jeffrey told me everything."

Douglas dismissed Kevin's words. "Jeffrey? That wimp? He had nothing to do with this."

"I know," said Kevin. "But you've been paying his cousin Patrick for years to spy on me through Jeff."

Krystal's voice cut through the room. "Silence!"

Everyone turned to look at her.

Krystal straightened her spine. "Douglas, this is not the time or place for one of your theatrical tantrums. Kevin and Megan are not the first young couple to sign a prenup."

Douglas's complexion reddened with anger. "This prenup spells out that this whole thing is a marriage of convenience!" He pointed his empty hand at Megan. "That money-grubbing gold digger spelled out exactly how Kevin is to pay off her medical bills."

Vernon Mully needed only three long strides to reach Douglas and one short, sharp jab to break his nose.

Blood spurted down the front of Douglas's white shirt.

"What the hell?! You son of a bitch!" Douglas pulled his arm back, telegraphing his intentions to the whole room.

Kevin had plenty of time to step between them and grab his father's arm before he could retaliate.

"Stop it!" warned Kevin quietly.

"I'll sue that man!"

Glenda Mully gasped and moved to stand beside her husband.

Krystal's tone cut like a knife. "No one is being sued. You're making a fool of yourself, Douglas. Do you think you're the only one with a team of lawyers?" She glanced about and caught the eye of one of the three suits who had been huddling with Kevin in the corner. "Mr. Ratigan? Will you please put an end to this display so these young people can get on with their wedding?"

The eldest of the group of lawyers stepped forward and cleared his throat.

"I am not quite sure which point of the situation you wish me to comment upon, Mrs. Wake."

"Oh, cut the lawyer crap and tell them what you told me this morning," said Krystal.

Ratigan's brows shot up. "Very well, then. For the benefit of Mr. Wake the younger and his bride, let me say first that Mr. Douglas Wake is objecting to today's nuptials based on the existence of a prenuptial agreement that spells out certain financial arrangements and obligations that both signees agreed to prior to their marriage. Such agreements are not uncommon, and in fact in most cases I wholeheartedly advocate—"

"Dennis! Spit it out," said Krystal.

"Yes, yes, of course. To the crux of the matter. Mr. Wake the elder is objecting because he believes the existence of said prenup violates the requirement of the Fineman family trust."

Douglas was pressing a blood-soaked handkerchief to his nose. His voice was muffled. "Of course it does! The trust demands a legitimate marriage prior to the heir's twenty-fifth birthday. The prenup proves they didn't love each other. They entered into this arrangement for the sole purpose of acquiring possession of the trust."

Dennis Ratigan's narrow mouth twitched in a small smile of triumph. "Considering the admirable team of legal advisors you have assembled, I find it hard to believe that they have not explained this situation to you in very clear terms."

Megan moved forward to stand by Krystal.

"Mrs. Wake, please sit down," she said softly. "I'll stand for both of us."

Krystal balanced herself on Megan's arm and sat gratefully.

Megan continued, "Mr. Ratigan, for those of us who do not have a team of lawyers, please explain what you're talking about."

Ratigan cleared his throat again. "Very well. The requirements of this trust were established long ago. At that time, it was common for—"

Kevin and Krystal chorused, "Get to the point!"

Ratigan looked miffed, but he complied. "There is no requirement that the bride and groom be in love. Merely that they be married."

Douglas dabbed at his nose. The bleeding had stopped. He sounded like a man with a bad cold. "Well, they aren't going to make that deadline either. By marrying today, a Friday, that license won't be filed until Monday. Am I right?" He looked to his legal trio for support.

"Wrong," said Kevin. He pulled a folded paper out of his inside coat pocket and held it in the air. "You were betting against me, dad. You wanted me to fail. You were counting on my dislike of your business practices and our personal differences to keep me from taking action. Well, I'm not eighteen anymore. And I'm not single anymore either. Megan and I were married in Nevada four days ago."

Glenda Mully cried out in surprise and clapped her hands.

Krystal allowed herself a satisfied twinge of a smile.

Zach stepped forward and shook Kevin's hand. "Congratulations four days late."

Kevin grinned.

Douglas's color now matched his nose. He looked ready to pop. At last he blustered, "I need a doctor! You three, come with me!" He ushered his legal team toward the door, but one of them turned long enough to address Ratigan.

"Just so you know, we've been telling him all along that he didn't have a leg to stand on."

Douglas's voice boomed, "You're fired!"

The guests were buzzing.

Krystal tugged at Megan's arm.

"Yes, Mrs. Wake?"

"My dear, I think it's time for you to marry your true love."

Megan beamed. "I agree." She held her elbows akimbo. "Dad? Zach? Are you ready to walk me down the aisle?"

Glenda returned to the Wurlitzer with an, "Oh, goody!" She began playing the "Wedding March" again.

Kevin put the marriage certificate back in his pocket and took his place before the minister. Jeffrey stood nearby as his best man.

Kevin's mouth dropped open and he slapped his forehead.

"Rings!" he cried. "I never had time to buy the rings!"

Keegan appeared with a black velvet box.

"They're right here," he said. "Zach gave 'em to me."

Kevin turned a questioning glance toward Zach, who raised his eyes to the ceiling and said nothing.

Krystal smiled softly. "I wondered for years if you'd taken them back for a refund."

"No, ma'am," said Zach. "I figured if I waited long enough, they would come in handy."

The ceremony was brief, but Megan was sure there was no one in the room who would ever forget her wedding day.

Chapter Fifty-Three

TWO MONTHS LATER, Kevin hung up the phone. Megan waited at the kitchen table to hear the news. Cookie tried to pretend she wasn't listening.

"The check cleared the bank," he said. "Your medical bills are history!"

"Yay!" Megan threw her arms around his neck. "Thank you so much," she whispered.

Karla and Keegan tramped into the room, followed by Chunky and Creamy, who were nearly twice as large at five months as they'd been at three.

Karla said, "Ew, get a room." She was wearing black shorts and a black tank top, but her face, arms and legs were showing a very unvampirelike tan.

Keegan had sun streaks in his brown hair, and he was growing almost as fast as the pups. His second grade jeans were now two inches above his ankles.

"Mom says we have to go shopping for school clothes today," he said. "But we can get ice cream when we're done!"

Kevin and Megan looked at Karla. She shrugged. "Vampires have to eat."

Kevin grinned. "I take it you're okay with the idea of going to school in Colorado?"

Karla tried to look glum. "I'll have to spread the vampire message to my new classmates, but I guess it'll be okay. Mom says I should go incognito, you know, dress like my prey for the first few weeks. Sounds like a good plan."

Krystal called from the parlor. "Kids! Come on, Glenda's ready to go!"

"It's so nice of your mother to help Krystal like this," said Kevin.

"Are you kidding? She's thrilled! Mom said she could never repay your family for steering dad to his own little church in Eagle's Toe."

"Did the board really limit him to one hellfire sermon a month?"

Megan nodded. "And they decided at last night's board meeting that they're going to invite motivational speakers at least once a month. So dad can be semi-retired, and mom can stay close by. And that is really perfect."

Kevin smiled. "I know you missed her terribly while they were in Guatemala. I'm so busy with ranch business now, I'm glad you have company during the day."

"And it will come in very handy around April Fool's Day, as well."

"April Fool's Day?" Kevin looked puzzled.

Cookie quizzically looked over her shoulder. Then her eyes got big and she started counting on her fingers. With a whoop, she gave Megan a big hug.

"What?" asked Kevin. "What?!"

"How about a wager?" asked Cookie, grabbing her hot pad and taking a cookie sheet out of the oven. "I'll bet you an oven full of chocolate chip cookies that he doesn't figure it out before the nine months are up. Megan? Megan?"

She turned around, cookies in hand, but Megan couldn't answer.

Kevin had wrapped her up in a celebratory kiss.

About the Author

Regina Duke has walked the beaches of Spain, shared a Mexican shower with a four-inch-long cockroach, and heated her 10th floor British walk-up hotel room by running hot water in the bath! Back home in northern Nevada, she writes fiction from romance to cozy mystery to quiet horror and soft science fiction. Regina's alter-ego Linda White sometimes writes dog books about her talented papillons. They're earning titles in rally, obedience, agility, and tricks.

For fiction, please visit her at www.ReginaDuke.com. And for non-fiction, www.LindaLouWrites.com.

Made in the USA
San Bernardino, CA
12 December 2016